STUDENT

For Sue,
again and again

STUDENT

David Belbin

Five Leaves
Publications

Student
by David Belbin

Published in 2012 by
Five Leaves Publications,
PO Box 8786, Nottingham NG1 9AW
www.fiveleaves.co.uk

ISBN 978-1907869532

Five Leaves
acknowledges financial support
from Arts Council England

Typeset and designed by
Four Sheets Design and Print
Printed by Russell Press, Nottingham

2 4 6 8 10 9 7 5 3 1

CONTENTS

WAKING EARLY, WEST KIRBY

I have a hangover but that isn't what's stopping me from getting back to sleep. It's remembering. I go back over everything I did last night recalling pretty much every word said to me, every word I said back, to make sure I didn't make a fool of myself.

Only when I'm certain I did nothing stupid do I look at my watch. Half past five. I've slept less than four hours. Outside, the sun is beginning to bleed across the clear sky. I go downstairs, not caring how much noise I make. Every night, Mum takes two sleeping pills and is dead to the world until at least nine.

I scare my mother. She can't wait for me to go to university, presuming I get the grades. Then she can screw married men, sleep all day and drink a bottle of gin every night without anyone to answer to. I scare my father, too. He's had me to stay once since the divorce. I scare my friends, but at least they tell me why, some of them. I am too articulate, they say. I have this *look* that freezes them out. I take everything too seriously. I always have to be in control.

I scare myself sometimes. *Lighten up*, Mark says to me. *You need to lighten up*. He acts like he cares, but that's probably because he wants to sleep with me. This is something my friends and I used to discuss a lot. How boys only act interested because they want sex. Why did we stop talking about that? Too obvious? No. Everyone states the obvious, all the time. It's because we're all sleeping with our boyfriends now. Except me.

I smell of smoke, sweat and stale perfume. Later, when the water's hot enough, I'll have a bath. In the meantime, I dress and leave the house, walk up Beacon Hill and cross the road into The Common. It's my favourite part of this place, The Common. If you walk far enough, it takes you to the sea. Earlier in the summer, I'd take my books and walk to the part where the trees are at their densest, nearly blocking out the sky. I'd find a hollow to burrow into and I'd read, read until I couldn't absorb any more. Then I'd go to the beach and walk up and down until my head was clear and I was ready to revise again.

The Common is the quietest I've ever known it. Too early for the dog-walkers, even. There's a sea breeze and I feel stupid for wearing only a short-sleeved T-shirt. I go down the hill and decide to sit for a while, think. I find a familiar hollow and curl up in it. A sharp stone pokes my thigh. I move it. Then I think about sex.

I wouldn't mind doing it with someone, just to get it over with. But the only boy I feel safe asking is Mark, and we have history. If we had sex, it wouldn't be casual. This is the wrong time for us to get serious. Mark's going to Cardiff. I'll be in Nottingham. They're too far apart. So we've agreed to split up, even though we never really agreed that we were going out. Thinking about this gives me a dark, heavy feeling at the back of my head. Within minutes, I'm asleep.

I'm woken by heavy footsteps, close by. I check my watch. Quarter to seven. Who walks at this time on a Monday? This isn't a short cut to anywhere. I don't hear a dog. Still, if I have a right to be here this early, so does the walker.

The hollow I'm in is on one of two overgrown slopes, facing each other, with a path running between them. A man is coming down the path very slowly, clumsily. I recognise him. His name is Bob Pritchard. He went out with my mum a few times. I go to the Grammar School with his daughter, Zoe.

Bob weaves in and out of the trees. He's drunk, I figure, and hasn't been home yet. He stops to relieve himself and I look away. I realise I'm hungry and thirsty and the water's been on for an hour, so I can have my bath. As soon as Bob leaves, I'll go home. But Bob doesn't seem in a hurry to go. He's leaning on a tree. As I watch, he begins to bang his head against the bark, slowly. I think he might be crying. I watch him do this for a long time then think *sod it* and get up to go. I'm sure that Bob won't notice me, but he does.

'Hey!' His voice is loud, authoritative. 'I want to talk to you!'

Bob, no longer so clumsy, is pushing branches aside, coming up the hill. This ground isn't made for fast escapes. There are big bushes and trees and pitted earth between me and the ridge. Before I can decide what to do, Bob's in front of me.

'How long were you watching me?'

His voice is slightly slurred.

'I haven't been watching. I've been asleep.'

'Aah. Out for the night, were you?'

I don't reply.

'You're Kathy's daughter.'

Reluctantly, I nod. He smiles lecherously.

'Do you take after your mother?'

'Go away,' I mouth, but no words come out.

'I'll bet you were a bad girl last night.'

When I reply, I sound like Mum: 'Ask your daughter. She was there.'

And she was the one being the bad girl, though I don't say this. Bob's still blocking the way down to the path. I decide to brazen it out, walk past him.

As I come towards him, Bob makes a whimpering noise. 'She threw me out last night,' he explains, almost pleads. 'I had to spend the night here.'

Close up, Bob reminds me of my father, a seedy, middle class, middle-aged, middle-management man. He probably got thrown out for fucking around once too often, like my dad did.

'Go home,' I say. 'She's probably changed her mind.'

Bob gives me a sickening smile. 'You're a kind girl,' he says. 'You do take after your mother.'

Out of some polite habit, I smile, then try to pass him. That's when he grabs me. A moment later I'm on the ground, pinned down by his heavy body.

'You're a kind girl,' he repeats.

I try to kick him but can't move my legs. Bob uses his free hand to grab at my jeans. I cry out. It's more like a yelp than a scream, but there's nobody around to hear me anyhow. That's when Bob punches me in the stomach, hard. Then, while I'm winded, he pulls up my T-shirt, ripping it. He pushes a wad of T-shirt into my mouth and I think — *he's done this before.*

We're in the hollow where I was asleep. What's happening can't be seen from the path below. With one hand, Bob holds me down, while the other tugs at my jeans until they're around my knees. Bob grimaces, realising that he needs both hands to unbuckle his belt. In this fraction of freedom, I reach for the rock I moved earlier, the one that was digging into my thigh.

'You're going to enjoy this,' Bob pants and, before he can press down on me again, I smash the rock against his head. Warm blood splashes my cheek and shoulder. His head flops sideways, above mine. Bob doesn't move. I realise he's unconscious. Now I need all my strength to push him off me. I take the torn T-shirt out of my mouth before looking at him. He's on his side, not breathing.

I start shivering and pull up my jeans. The T-shirt is hanging off my chest, exposing my left breast. Bob still isn't moving. The bloody rock is by his head. A half bottle of whisky pokes out of his jacket pocket. I think about all the questions I will have to answer, all the things that people will say. What was I doing on The Common at seven in the morning? How well did I know Bob Pritchard? How long have I been seeing him?

The pool of blood around Bob's head is growing. I do what they taught me in Brownies. I look for his pulse. I think I find one, but it's very faint. I don't have my mobile with me. There's a phone box fifteen minutes walk away. Ten if I run. But then the questions will start.

This decision will affect the rest of my life. It's not deciding whether to get off with someone you only half like at a party. Whatever I choose to do, I'll go over my motives and my reasoning again and again. And the decision has to be made now. Someone might come along at any minute. Part of my mind is numb, in shock. Another part schemes.

The only thing I've touched is the rock. I pick it up and look around, making sure I've left no traces of myself. Then I hurry down to the path. I walk fast, keeping to the side so I can duck behind a bush if anybody approaches. I pass the tall black beacon that gives my street its name. Now for the difficult bit. My left hand is on my shoulder, holding my T-shirt in place. The right holds the rock, beneath the T-shirt, over my belly. I leave The Common looking like a pregnant urchin.

My luck holds. There's nobody on the street. The milkman's been and gone. I let myself into the house, where I put my T-shirt in with the wash, turn the machine on. I rinse the bloody rock in hot, hot water and open the back door. I hurl the murder weapon into the rockery. Then I run myself a bath. It's not quite as deep as I like, because the washing machine has already used a lot of the hot water. But by the time I get out, all the evidence is gone. I'm clean.

I spend the next four days waiting for someone to say something about Bob Pritchard. The local paper isn't out until Friday, so I start listening to Radio Merseyside news bulletins. Nothing. Maybe they haven't found the body yet. I think about walking across The Common, checking whether Bob's where I left him. But that would be stupid: the killer returning to the scene of the crime. I daren't ring Zoe Pritchard, either. We're not that good friends. To phone out of the blue would be suspicious.

Thursday is the day of the A-level results. You can turn up at school from midday onwards and get the results in person or have them posted to arrive the next day. Mark rings and I agree to go with him. We wait until one, hoping to avoid the queue, the crowd.

I get the grades I need, Mark doesn't. On our way out, he

begins to chatter about what a wonderful time I'm going to have in Nottingham. I want to go to bed with Mark right this minute, I'm so sorry for him. Then I see Zoe Pritchard.

She's on the street with a bunch of people who are discussing their results. And she's crying. The guy she was with last Sunday night tries to comfort her but Zoe brushes him off. I'm the only one who knows: it isn't her grades she's crying about, it's her dad. For the first and last time, I feel guilty about what I've done. Not for hitting him, I had to do that. But I should have called an ambulance.

Zoe's mum gets out of the car and goes over to her. Mrs Pritchard looks heartbroken too. They hug each other. I ought to go over. I ought to say something, though I've no idea what. I hang back, watching Zoe and her mum return to their car. Mrs Pritchard gets into the driver's seat. Zoe tries to get in the back, finds the door locked. An arm reaches back to open it and I realise there's somebody in the front passenger seat.

Bob Pritchard kisses his daughter, who is careful not to make contact with the big bandage covering the back and side of his head. As she's doing this, Bob looks over his shoulder and sees me. Before our eyes can meet, he turns back.

Then his wife drives away.

CHRISTMAS EVE

'Why haven't you been back before?' Mark asks. 'Everyone else has.'

Half the students I know go home every weekend. They eat well, get their washing done, see friends. But most of my West Kirby friends have just started university, so won't be around. My mum's not much of a cook and the journey home takes four hours. I explain some of this.

'You could have come to see me,' I conclude.

'It's not so easy.'

Since I left West Kirby, Mark works most weekends at the golf club, even in winter. This allows him to attend college, prepare for retakes. But he could come to see me in the week. I suspect Mark thinks he'll feel out of place at uni. I do. I like it best at weekends, when none of the lecturers are around, and there are far fewer students. Mostly it's overseas students and misfits like me, people with nothing to go home for.

'I'm here now, anyway,' I say. 'Miss me?'

'What do you think?' This should be the point for a hug, but I don't get one. My fault. We finished our on-off thing because it wasn't fair to tie each other down when we were going to be apart for three years (though Mark could have applied to go to Nottingham, too. Or Leicester, Loughborough, Sheffield, somewhere within easy reach. But he chose Cardiff, a ridiculous distance away. Then he didn't get the grades he needed anyway.)

Mark gives me the hangdog look that made me go out with him in the first place. I kiss him, a gentle peck on the cheek. That's when he tells me.

'I'm going out with Helen.'

'Helen Kent?' Pause. Polite reaction. 'Right. Good for you.'

Helen was in the year below me at school. She's tall, an Amazon, the sort of girl other girls were always getting a crush on.

'She's out of my league, really, but she's into golf and, you know, I started giving her lessons.'

'Nice,' is all I can think of to say.

'I reckon the two of you will get on.'

'Uh huh.' We'll have to, if Mark is to remain my best friend.

'I'll make some coffee.'

Mark leaves me in his purple walled bedroom. All over the world, I reflect, students are coming back from their first term at university and dumping their hometown boy or girlfriends. For a moment there, I'd meant to do the opposite, tell Mark I'd seen the competition and it was him I wanted, with his shaggy hair, dopey smile and comfortable, reassuringly male odour. But he has snagged Helen of Troy.

When he's returned with the coffee, Mark rolls a joint. He always has better dope than anyone else, gets it at the golf club. Don't know who from. Dope takes me deeper into myself, but it doesn't help me open up about what I find there. Mark asks whether I'm seeing anyone. I shake my head.

'Guys in Nottingham are just the same as guys here. Immature. Present company excepted, of course.'

'You always said you got on better with boys than with girls.'

'I do. Except for the ones who want to go out with me.'

'Present company excepted?'

'I've always thought of you more as a friend than a lover,' I fib.

'I noticed.'

I give him a sheepish smile. I nearly slept with Mark, several times, but I wanted to be sure before I lost my virginity. Stupid. Nobody's ever sure. We were together eight months and he deserved more than a couple of inept blow jobs. I'll bet Helen Kent gives him whatever he wants. I say none of this. I keep thinking about how Bob Pritchard was nearly my first and I wish I'd succumbed to Mark long, long before that horrible morning, which I keep trying to erase from my memory.

After a while, I announce that I have the munchies and demand my usual hall of residence late night snack: peanut butter on digestive biscuits washed down with a large glass of cold milk.

'You'll get fat,' he teases as I wolf it down.

'I wish,' I say, pointing at my tummy, which is not so much flat as concave. Mark always claimed to love my small bottom and tiny tits, but now he's going out with Wonder Woman so I suspect he was exaggerating.

I have to go home. My dad's picking me up to spend Christmas Eve with him, his second wife, and my two-year-old half brother. Stoned, I think I can face them. I haven't seen

Dad since the day after the exam results, when he was so pleased with my three As that he promised me a car, even though I don't know how to drive. I ask Mark whether he'll come round on Boxing Day, but he ducks the question.

'I'll ring you,' he says.

The world has changed. He has to consult Helen first. Mark sees me to the door and kisses me goodbye on the forehead. Once, he would have offered to walk me home.

I spent last Christmas Eve at Mark's. His parents went to Midnight Mass but didn't insist we went with them. When they got back, all smiles and mince pies, they gave me a lift home. I found Mum asleep on the sofa, bottle by her side. I couldn't wake her and wasn't strong enough to drag her to bed.

Dad's second wife, Ingrid, is thirty. When I was born, she was eleven or twelve. It doesn't seem natural. I mean, it *is* natural, but it's equally natural that I don't want to see her, or my half brother. And it occurs to me, stoned, as I float home along dull suburban streets, that I don't have to see them. I don't even have to see Dad, who walked out on me, as well as Mum, the year before I did my GCSEs. In fact, fuck it. I won't.

Back at Beacon Drive, Mum has already gone out. She's left a note saying 'dinner at four tomorrow'. If last year is anything to go by, this is wildly optimistic. I find a small turkey in the fridge, alongside several bottles of white wine, not all of them cheap. At least she's making an effort.

I wonder who Mum's spending the evening with. She never discusses her love life, nor me mine. This being Christmas Eve, her date's unlikely to be married, but I wouldn't put anything past her.

I write a note for Dad and put it on the door. In my room,

I wait for him to come and go. While I'm waiting, I think about Mark and Helen. I'm jealous. There's no point in denying that to myself, no matter how stoned I am. I want to hurt someone and the only person I can hurt is Dad. I imagine him banging on the door, insisting I accompany him to his detached dream house in Meols, a wedding present from his wealthy new in-laws.

I pour myself some wine. Half a glass. Nearly everyone I know spends their free time getting off their face. I'd like to be the same, but don't like to lose control. Dope relaxes me. Too much, maybe. I'm sure Mark failed his exams because he smoked too much weed. That's the biggest reason I didn't sleep with him. Weed made him laid back and cerebral. He didn't pressure me to let him into my knickers. If he'd begged more, I would have caved.

I want to put some sounds on, lose myself in music, but I also want to hear Dad come and go. I've put the lights in my room on full, so he'll know I'm in. I want to hear him react to what I've written in the note pinned to the front door. I look at my watch. He's twenty minutes late. The wine's gone. Bracing myself for the effort involved in ignoring him, I make myself a large gin and tonic. Mum always has two fingers of gin. I settle for one.

I don't want to be a virgin. At uni, only the Christian girls are saving it and you can already see them beginning to have doubts. Everyone else got it over with before arriving or failing that, during fresher week. Some lads came on to me then, too, but nobody tried hard enough. There was always someone round the corner who would offer less resistance.

The phone rings. I check that Dad isn't outside before answering it.

When I come off the phone, thirty seconds later, I add the second finger of gin to my drink. So what if his wife and son are both ill, it's me Dad doesn't want to see. When he started to go on about rescheduling for next week, I hung up.

I make another drink. And another. I decide that I really, really want to smoke some more dope. It'll chill me out. But I don't have any. I only know one person who definitely does and he's probably with Helen. She'll be round at his, like I was last year. I'm far too proud to ring him.

I'll run myself a bath instead. That always relaxes me. Or I'll buy some cigarettes. I sometimes smoke when I'm drunk, though I know it's the start of a slippery slope.

After finishing my third gin and tonic, when there's nothing on TV, I ring Mark. He drives round in his mum's car. I didn't even know he'd passed his test, that's how out of touch I am. I'm sorry, though, that he's driven, because it means he won't have a drink and getting him intoxicated is the only device I have to get him into bed. I refuse to cry because my dad abandoned me on Christmas Eve. I refuse to.

'I can't believe what a bastard he is,' Mark says. 'It's no wonder your mother...' Tactfully, he doesn't finish the sentence. Instead, he hugs me.

When I finish crying, I wash my face. Mark makes coffee. I don't think he can tell how much I've had to drink, how much Dutch courage I needed before I could bring myself to call him. He rolls me a couple of joints, explaining that he'd better not smoke, since he's driving.

'But don't let me stop you,' he says, handing over a fat one.

I shake my head. 'We'd better find something else to do.'

Mark gives me one of his silly, lop-sided grins. I take him

by the hand and lead him upstairs. I'm worried that at any point he'll stop, mention Helen. He doesn't say anything. We undress each other like it's the most natural thing in the world. He makes love to me gently. It hardly hurts at all. I'm sorry I'm so drunk, because I want to remember this, I want to experience it fully. I've waited a long time to find out what it feels like to have somebody else inside me.

If Mark is surprised I'm still a virgin he doesn't say. Or maybe he can't tell, thinks that the blood is from my period. After he's taken the condom off, he holds me.

'We should have done that this time last year,' I say.

'I only ever get things when I give up hoping for them,' he tells me.

There's no self-pity in his words, but they make me uncomfortable.

'So much for hope,' is all I can think of to say.

At ten thirty, Mum comes crashing in. We listen as she goes to bed, not realising I'm home. I want Mark to make love to me again but he has to go. He needs to get the car back to his parents for Midnight Mass.

'You're great, Allison,' he tells me. 'Too great to stay round here. Too great to let your dad get to you.'

After he's gone, I keep thinking about Helen Kent, wondering if he went from me to her. Downstairs, I smoke one of the joints he left behind but stub it out halfway because I'm about to flake out.

When I wake on Christmas morning, I'm a little sore. It takes a couple of moments for me to remember why. While my bath is running, I put the oven on for the turkey.

SECOND TERM

Mark has had several months in which to visit, but now his girlfriend has an interview at Nottingham and he's dropping everything to drive her over. We arrange to meet for lunch, after my midday lecture. Mark's confident he can find Mooch, even though he's never been to the city before. When I turn up, he's already waiting at the bar, drinks bought, big grin on his face, telling me I look good, even though I've let my hair grow over my neck and he likes it short, or used to.

'Is it right what they say, that you spend your most of your first year getting rid of the friends you made in your first term?'

I consider correcting the quotation, providing what I think is the right attribution (my mum has the *Brideshead Revisited* box set) but manage to restrain myself. Back in Sixth form, Mark was often on at me to 'tone down my act', not scare people off with my intelligence. Whereas I was looking for people to compete with me. At university, I thought I'd make friends who'd want to debate and dissect. But those soulmates only exist in Oxbridge novels. Here, everyone wants to get trashed all the time, just like at home.

'I didn't make that many friends in my first term,' I tell Mark. 'You know how I am. I don't make friends easily.'

He looks concerned so I burble on. 'I mean, I know loads of people. I'm not lonely or anything.'

'Or anything,' he repeats, an old trick of his to get me to expand on what I've said without actually questioning me.

'Allison!' Cate West, from my corridor. 'Did you hear that noise at two this morning. I thought...' She notices Mark and brazenly looks him up and down, liking what she sees. 'Where has Allison been keeping you hidden?'

'Merseyside. I'm visiting.'

'Allison's so mysterious. She never let on she had someone at home.'

'She dumped me last summer. But we're still mates.'

'I *didn't* dump you,' I protest. 'It was mutual — more or less.' Then I direct my dagger eyes at Cate. 'Actually, we've got a lot of catching up to do and Mark's only got a couple of hours.'

Cate raises one eyebrow. '*Sor-ree.*'

As she flounces off, Mark frowns, then shakes his head. 'That's the reason you haven't got many friends.'

I kick him affectionately in the ankle. He kicks me back.

'How's Helen?' I want to know.

'You can ask her yourself.'

'I'd love to, but I have a seminar at two.'

'She'll be here before that. She really wants to talk to you. She's serious about coming here.'

'You can tell her what I've told you.'

'You haven't told me anything yet. You haven't even told me if you've got a boyfriend.'

'That's a non-sequitur,' I tell him, although I know this is key information for Helen. She will feel much more comfortable about my seeing Mark if I have a new bloke in tow. Maybe I should find a malleable gay man from central casting who will charm Helen so much she fails to notice that I'm winning Mark back. Only I don't want to win him back. What good is an on-off boyfriend back home? I'd like to sleep with him again. I'd like to sleep with someone. Having sex just once feels like a cruel trick I've played on myself — better not to have found out that I liked it.

'There's nobody serious,' I add. 'You know how hard I am to get close to.'

'You know how close I am to getting hard,' Mark says, another old gag, but one that doesn't sit well with me this afternoon.

'How are your retakes going?'

'It's not going to be a problem,' Mark says. 'Long as I get a C in English Lit, I'm in.'

'In where? Cardiff again?'

'No. Nottingham. The other place. Trent. Why do you think Helen's applied here?'

I want to punch him. He never showed any interest in coming to Nottingham when we were going out.

'I did a really good job of selling the city, did I?'

'I always fancied it. Before, I'd have felt funny, following you here. But since we split up, I thought *why not?*'

'And Helen doesn't think it's odd, coming to the same city as you?'

'We want to stay together.'

'Don't you think it might be a bit weird, the two of you starting university at the same time, in the same place, but on a different campus?'

'Don't see why. We've been together six months. That's more than you and me managed — consecutively, anyway.' This last with a wry grin. 'But we won't be on top of each other. Also, if things don't work out, it's not as though we'll run into each other all the time.'

'You really have thought it through.'

'I'm serious about her. I want you to be friends with her. Hey, look. It's our turn on the pool table.'

Mark had left money on the pool table, booking us a turn. It's not like in the pubs at home, where the winner stays on and challengers put the money in. Mark, being Mark, has sussed out the system before I got here. I let him break. We used to play a lot of pool. It's a good way to get around not having enough to talk about when you want to stay in the pub all evening. And it's a good way to avoid talking about what he's just told me.

We have never spoken about or referred to what happened on Christmas Eve. Mark did me a favour, that's how I try to think about it. Your first time ought to be with someone you care about. What happened between us was an epilogue, a way of wrapping up my relationship with him, which lasted most of the upper sixth, if you don't count the times when I was trying to dump him. We were together longer than six months, by the way. More like a year.

We're down to two balls each when Helen arrives, early. Her interview has gone well. She asks no-brainer questions about the university while I try to beat her boyfriend at pool. I answer impatiently. It's obvious her experience will be different to mine. Look at her, nearly six feet tall with the sort of breasts other women have to pay for. She's a walking advert for the National Health Service and the wonderbra. Even soberly dressed for interview, she's a sex-bomb. Also she's warm and friendly, all the things I'm not. When Helen asks a question, it's because she's interested in the answer rather than because she enjoys interrogating people (this isn't how I feel but it's the impression I give, according to a carefully balanced selection of my friends and enemies). People will queue up to be Helen's friend.

Mark lets me win and goes off to buy another drink, even though I try to insist it's my round. Helen and I pretend to bond.

'I used to be so jealous of you going out with Mark when I was in the lower sixth,' Helen says. 'I don't think he even noticed me until you left.'

I don't know how I appear to react to this, but Helen blunders on. 'Are you going to be all right with it next year, Mark being in the same city?'

Has Mark told her who dumped who? He probably said the same to her as I said to Cate, that it was mutual. Technically, though, I dumped him.

'People from the two universities don't mix much,' I tell her, wondering if she'll note the warning. Second years don't tend to mix much with first years, either, not at first, anyway — unless you count the ones who prey on sweet young virgins, a category Helen definitely doesn't belong to. 'It's really not a problem for me.'

'Great. I hope we can be friends. If I get in here, I mean.'

'We can be friends anyway,' I assure her.

She's waiting for a freely given promise that I don't want Mark back, but she's not going to get it, and is too streetwise to ask. In a fair fight, she'll always win. Helen and Mark live six streets from each other. I'm a hundred and fifty miles away.

'Want another game?' Helen has already taken a coin out of her purse and released the balls.

'Hey!' Noises off.

25

'I think it was their turn to play,' I point out to her.

'Sorry,' she turns to them, all charm. 'Fancy a game of doubles, on me?'

'No, you're all right,' says a guy in an oversized woollen jumper.

'Are you sure? We don't bite, I promise.'

'All right then,' says his mate, who's wearing a combat jacket.

'Great,' Helen says, beaming, then, *sotto voce* to me. 'He's cute.'

Mark returns with the drinks and watches as the two women he's trained combine to slaughter the newcomers. The lads try to laugh it off, putting in their money for the next game and insisting on a rematch. But I have to go. As I'm saying goodbye to Mark I see Helen whisper something to combat jacket. He comes over.

'Your friend says it's OK to ask for your mobile number,' he says, sheepishly.

I try not to frown. He is quite cute. 'What's your name?' I say.

'Simon.'

'OK, Simon. I'm Allison.'

Do I like him? We have discussed nothing other than pool shots and I'm pretty sure he's a mechanical engineer. I give him my number anyway.

At the door, Mark kisses me goodbye, on the forehead. Helen leans forward to give me a hug.

'I'm going to forgive you for what you and Mark got up to at Christmas,' she whispers in my ear. 'Mark says it was a one off.'

'I'm sorry,' I say. 'I was... upset.'

'You don't have to make excuses,' Helen tells me. 'He's

already eaten his humble pie.' She turns to Mark, who's looking decidedly queasy. 'At least he had the guts to tell me. See you at Easter.'

I nod, then hurry out of the Portland Building with my head down, humiliated at being so outclassed by somebody from the year below.

Later, after several more games of pool and three pints of cider, I go to bed with Simon. I want to capture some spark of what I felt with Mark on Christmas Eve. Or what I wish I think I felt. I was too drunk for me to remember much beyond the closeness and the long-imagined sensation of having him inside me. This time, it's over in seconds and Simon can't wait to get out of my room. I could sense it, all the time I was with him: he wanted me to be Helen. But that's fair enough, because I wanted him to be Mark.

FRIENDS

One life slips into another. These days, West Kirby's merely the place I visit during vacations. It's hard to be bothered that Zoe Pritchard has dropped out of uni and is working in the travel agents, or that some guy I barely knew at school crashed his car. I went out with Mark just once over Easter break. Helen was too busy to join us: revising, supposedly. I tried to get Mark to come round again, when Mum was away with some bloke, but he said he was working six days of the week at the golf club, getting up ridiculously early. I ended up doing half an e with Zoe instead. Her parents were away so I didn't have to think much about bastard Bob. We got trashed on skunk and watched shit on satellite TV. God, I'm glad to be back in Nottingham.

Mark asked if I was seeing anyone. Too proud to tell the truth, too honest to lie, I said there was somebody on my corridor interested in me, but I wasn't sure about them. What I didn't tell Mark was that the interested party was female. Though that might have turned him on.

Now we're back, all the talk in hall is of 'next year' and who's going to live with whom. I like hall, but only saddoes stay for a second year. Half the people you talk to have already sorted out a house share in Dunkirk or Lenton with their 'bessie mates'. Nobody's asked me. That is, several people have asked me what I'm doing next year and I've shrugged or hinted (perhaps not strongly enough) that I'm open to offers. But I haven't had any offers. Except from Vic.

Vic, short for Victoria, comes from a small town in Derbyshire where there's no gay scene whatsoever. Until uni, she'd had a couple of boyfriends who made her think she was frigid. In her second week here, she let a girl pick her up at a dive in town and had her first orgasm. She's been having one nighters with women ever since, but now she wants a relationship and I'm her chosen love object. She can't handle a relationship with the sort of woman she meets in town, she says. I think she's looking for a mirror image. We're the same height (5'4"), brown hair with blue eyes. OK, my chest is flatter than hers and her face is flatter than mine, but if we cut our hair the same way, you could take us for sisters. In bad light.

'Have you ever thought about sleeping with another woman?' Vic asks over late night coffee (decaf).

'Thought about it. I've also thought about murder and masochism, doesn't mean I'm interested in trying them.'

'Why not? Shouldn't you try everything that doesn't hurt anyone?'

'In theory, sure. In practice, you have to fancy someone first.'

Vic takes the hint and doesn't use the 'time to experiment' line again. A week later, she suggests that we share a flat together. I tell her I'm flattered but don't think it'll work.

'People will assume we're a couple. That'd cramp both our styles.'

'Let them assume what they want. We'll have a great time.'

I change my argument. 'There are hardly any two-bed places to be had and they cost the earth, Vic. It's not that I wouldn't like to live with you. If we had enough people for a shared house, perhaps...'

'I'll sort it,' she says.

Like me, Vic gets on fine with people in hall and has friends on her course but nobody she's anxious to form a second, replacement family with. And that's how most of the house hunters seem to see their future.

'Time's running out,' Vic says a day later. 'A lot of the best houses are already gone. We should start checking out notice-boards.'

'OK,' I say, comforted at having a partner in this quest, although neither of has much idea what we're searching for.

Nobody's sweating end of year exams, except me. They're pass/fail and the marks don't count towards your final degree result. I've always been anal about passing exams but, this year, I have a bigger priority: I want to get a boyfriend before Helen and Mark show up in the autumn. I've been for drinks with a couple of guys on my course. Nothing came of them. The nearest I've come to having sex lately was when a lad from the floor above me almost knocked me over when he was coming back from the pub the other night. He apologised and asked me if I'd like to sleep with him. I said ask me again when I'm sober. He hasn't.

But I'm not that desperate. At a hall party last weekend, I went back to what I thought was a girl's room to smoke some weed, but the girl (name forgotten) disappeared into the adjoining room and I found myself with a long-haired biker type, who gave me a slim line of coke, then got his prick out and asked me to lick it. I was out of there faster than you can say *eeugh*. I had other offers that night but the coke made me edgy and I think I must have slagged off the guys who tried to chat me up. I had to drink loads before I came down enough to sleep. Vic says I was advocating compulsory castration for even the mildest forms of sexual harassment.

'I don't think speed agrees with you,' Vic told me.

'He said it was coke.'

'I know that greaser. He's too hard up to fork out for coke. It would have been sulphate.'

'Perhaps I'd better avoid both in future.'

'I would if I were you. You turned pretty scary.'

May's nearly over. The exams are a week away and neither of us have a place to live next year. Vic knows this guy called Paul. They met at Gaysoc. He seems all right and is in the same position as us, but three's an even more awkward number. There are small houses we could rent a fair way out, in places like Long Eaton, but the ones near University Park all have five or six bedrooms. Vic and I go to an agency, who offer us bedsits: city centre, purpose-built, pile-'em-high, student cages. Paul contacts an old school Asian landlord who has houses in Lenton. There's one, he's told, where only a couple of people are staying on next year. We say we'll see it that evening.

The Derby Road runs from the university to the edge of the city, a long, steep hill. Albert Grove is near the top, in Lenton Sands. We get there early and walk past the house, which is halfway down on the left, to the pub, the Old Peacock, at the bottom of the street. There are a few shops, including a supermarket and a chippy.

'This could suit,' Paul says.

We agree to check out the pub after we've seen the house.

The guy who lets us in has a beard and a slight stoop, probably due to his height. He's at least a foot taller than me.

'Mr Soar told me to expect you,' he says. 'Shall I make us a brew while we wait for him?'

He's a second year called Finn. I want to quiz him about why he hasn't got three mates of his own to invite into the house. While I'm trying to think of a tactful way to do this, Vic wades in.

'You say three people are leaving. Why haven't you got some mates lined up to move in?'

'Tess is a fourth year medic, like me. Our friends have already got houses.'

My mother would be impressed if she knew I was living with doctors, even trainee ones.

'Can you take us round?' Paul asks.

'I don't suppose the others would mind.'

The house is on the shabby side of dingy. Finn explains that he and Tess plan to move into the two downstairs rooms next year. We nod as though this is the most natural thing in the world, although I'm not sure I'd want a front-facing, ground floor bedroom. At the moment, the front room seems to be a living room, with a sofa, telly and DVD player.

The landlord arrives when we're up in the attic room, which isn't too big, but has a skylight and a window looking out onto the street and the house opposite. You can lean out and see who's at the front door. I want it.

'What do you think?' Mr Soar asks.

'How long can we have to think about it?' Paul wants to know.

'I show another group round tomorrow evening,' Mr Soar says. If you call my mobile before then, the rooms are yours. 'If not...'

He shrugs theatrically. We would like to meet Tess, our other putative housemate, but she's not back from university yet, Finn says. He gives us his mobile number, so we can call him if there's anything else we want to know, then we go down to the pub to talk it over.

It's one of those pubs that must have once been a proper local only now students have taken it over, on both sides of the bar. The beer is cheap and so is the food. There's a queue for the pool table. As Paul is buying the drinks, I over-hear the people at the next table.

'Think they'll have gone by now?' the woman says. I assume, wildly but, as it turns out, correctly, that they are talking about us.

'Give it another five minutes,' a bloke says.

Vic starts to say something. I put a finger to my lips and jerk my head in their direction.

'I hope he changed his socks before they turned up,' a bloke says.

'God, I won't miss the smell of his feet,' says the girl.

'How do you think Tessa stands it?' A second bloke asks. 'I was sitting next to him in the cinema last week. It was like stale gorgonzola wafting at me all evening. I nearly puked.'

'Tess told me she got him to wear odour eaters,' the girl says, 'but that doesn't work in bed. She has to change the sheets twice a week.'

'Is that why they're always down the laundrette? I assumed they were having lots of...'

'I thought Tessa was one of those women who liked to sit on the washing machine with her legs wide open when it was on full spin and, you know...' the first bloke says and the girl cackles loudly so that some people look round, which gives me an excuse to do the same. The second bloke, who has a goatee, isn't laughing. The first guy is squeezing the woman's knee beneath the table. These three look like medics, in that they're more middle class and seem better off than most students. They have a supercilious sheen that makes me want to smack them. I didn't get that vibe from Finn (or notice any smell coming from his feet). He's more of a hippy. And if Tess or Tessa goes out with him, presumably she's OK too. Paul returns with the drinks. Vic puts a finger to her mouth and hisses, 'Next table. The other people from the house.'

They've gone quiet. I'm consumed by an urge to confront them. Or at least embarrass them a little. I do that sometimes. Mark calls these my *fuckitall* moments.

'Excuse me,' I say, and the woman looks in my direction. She can't be more than two years older than me but her expression says I don't belong in her world. I haven't decided what I'm going to say to her. Vic and Paul are having kittens. They really want this house, I can tell.

'Do you live round here? Only we're thinking of moving up the hill.'

'Which road?' Guy number one wants to know.

'Albert Grove.'

'Good street,' he says. 'Not too busy. Some of them are used as cut throughs by, you know, commuters.'

'Which university are you at?' the woman asks.

'The one down the road.'

'It's walkable. Bit of a drag in winter.'

'I'm getting a car,' I say. 'That's the main thing I'm worried about. Is it likely to get broken into, nicked?'

'I'd get an alarm if I were you,' says bloke number one. 'I got my window smashed in once, but that could happen just about anywhere.'

'I guess you're right.'

They leave, without volunteering that they live up the road or offering us any unsolicited advice.

'Condescending prats,' Vic says.

'They seemed all right to me,' Paul responds. 'Why should they tell us any more than we asked?'

'Think they realised what we were doing here?' I ask.

'Don't suppose they care,' Paul says. 'So what do you reckon? House seems all right to me.'

'I'd like to meet Tessa,' Vic says.

'She's straight,' Paul says. 'Why do you care what she's like?'

'She might be a psycho.'

'Or a smelly foot fetishist,' I point out. 'I'd like to invite her and Finn down for a drink. Think she's back yet?'

Finn said earlier that he was expecting her. It's been twenty minutes. I dial his number.

'We're in the Old Peacock,' I say, 'talking about your house. We wondered if Tessa was back and we could buy you both a drink.'

He umms and ahs for a moment. 'Hang on, I'll speak to Tess.'

There's speech in the background. The other three must have just come back. Then Finn's back on the line. 'We'll be ten minutes.'

While we're waiting, we discuss our situation. We want this house, provided Tessa turns out to be halfway sane and Finn's feet don't turn out to be so toxic they drive us away before we've finished our drinks. Vic is keenest. Paul and I

35

spar over who gets the attic room.

'I need my privacy,' he says. 'I need to know that nobody's going to walk past my door and accidentally stumble in.'

'You're more likely to pick up drunken one night stands than I am. And you might have trouble getting them up the extra flight of stairs. Anyway, if you or Vic has the top room, I'll be woken up by your bedroom gymnastics.'

'Celibate, are you?' Paul teases.

'I don't do one nighters,' I lie, for the only sex I've had so far has been one night stands. 'And when I do have sex, I'm very quiet.'

Vic leans over and whispers, sotto voce. 'She doesn't have orgasms.'

Paul laughs and, before I can protest, Finn and Tessa walk in. Tessa is slight, despite her height, and wears a cheeky, face wrinkling grin which I at once suspect is permanent. Without it, she might be very pretty.

I buy the drinks. Pint for him. Diet Coke for her. When I return to the table, they're all deep in conversation.

'That *was* them, the other housemates,' Vic tells me on my return, as though we were in any doubt over the matter. 'Tessa just explained why there might be a bit of an atmosphere.'

I look at Tessa but it's Finn who speaks. 'Thing is, when we moved in together, Greg...'

'That's the one with the goatee,' Paul says.

'...and Tess were a couple. Then the other two — Jon and Kat — got together and that made things a bit awkward for me, being the singleton. Only, when Greg and Tess split up, she started seeing me and, for some reason, we became like *the villains of the house.* I didn't want to explain earlier because it sounds incredibly childish.'

Tessa looks embarrassed and I get the impression that the move from Greg to Finn wasn't quite as civilised as Finn has described. A bit of overlap there, I'll bet, although, if first impressions are enough to go by, she made the right choice.

'Jon and Kat are buying a house together and Greg's moving in as their lodger to help with the mortgage. Tess and I thought of getting a flat but it would cost a lot more than the house. Also, we like living with other people.' He turns to Tessa and she nods, reignites the grin. 'You three seem pretty cool.'

'Vic and I are both gay,' Paul says, in a slightly sanctimonious tone. 'So if you're going to have any problem with that...'

'God no,' Tessa says, revealing a Liverpudlian accent that I hadn't been expecting, and wiping the embarrassed grin from her face to reveal a serious, compassionate trainee doctor apologising for the slight pain her rectal examination is about to cause you. 'I mean, that's the perfect combination isn't it — one straight, two gay but of different sexes. It's really not a good idea, getting off with your housemates, if you can avoid it. Though Finn and me, we're not really coupley, honest.'

'So it's settled then,' Finn says. 'You'll ring Mr Soar?'

We agree that we'll ring Mr Soar.

'And we promise that none of us will change our sexualities or sleep with anybody in the house that we're not already sleeping with,' Paul says.

Vic and I exchange a cynical glance before raising our glasses.

'Cheers!'

KEEP YOUR DISTANCE

I'm not the sort of person who has parties. The last one was when I was thirteen, before my parents' marriage fell apart. Now Mum's gone to Spain for a fortnight with a man she met at Alcoholics Anonymous. She's guilty about missing my birthday.

'It's OK,' I tell her. 'Nineteen's not a big deal birthday.'

'Go crazy,' Mum says, knowing that I never would. 'There's not much for you to wreck. Just make sure you clean up afterwards.'

There's no booze in the house but Dad says he'll float me. He offered to keep guard in case gatecrashers turn the place into a crack den.

'I don't want a party,' I say on the phone. 'The idea of throwing one turns my stomach.'

When I see my mates, I keep quiet about Mum being away. Only Mark knows. I told him because I thought it might tempt him to come round. So far it hasn't worked. He was working at the golf club every day, saving up money for university (presuming he gets a 'C' or above in his English retake) and the holiday he's just taken Helen on. I'm working four days a week at the job centre in Hoylake and also saving up, theoretically, for a holiday. 'Theoretically' because I've got nobody to go with. Vic and I planned on doing something but she's skint. The other day she phoned to say there was a crisis.

'Paul's decided not to move in with us. Someone dropped out of another house and they offered it to him and there are some blokes there who he really gets on with. He said he would have rung you only he knows you'd give him a hard time.'

'Too right I would have done. What now?'

'I'll go to the accommodation office, maybe put some flyers on noticeboards. That's if you're happy to leave it with me.'

'I don't have much choice.' For a fleeting moment, I think of Mark, complaining about the cost of his hall of residence place and the inconvenience of living out at Clifton when Helen will be on the other side of the city. 'You'd better check with Tessa and Finn. They might know someone.'

'If they knew anyone, we wouldn't be moving in.'

I daydream of turning up in October to discover a handsome, long-haired prince who loves Kafka, PJ Harvey and me. Nearly nineteen years old and I still have girlish dreams that some guy will sweep me off my feet.

Zoe Pritchard rings to tell me she's having a party. Her parents are away so I don't have to worry about running into her dad. We've never been big mates and, after what happened a year ago, I meant to steer clear of her so — naturally — she's decided that she wants to pal up with me. Zoe lives on the other side of The Common, a short walk from the sea. I get a lift over with Joanne Ford. Once I would have walked, but after what happened last summer I'm not willing to risk a twilight stroll through The Common.

Joanne's dad drops us off. Zoe answers the door. She greets us with great enthusiasm and, when we get inside, I understand why. Her brother Dom's mates outnumber hers two to one. The male to female ratio is similar. You can count the number of single women on the fingers of one hand. If I can't pull tonight, there *is* something wrong with me.

Dominic Pritchard, the proud possessor of a lower second in Chemistry, kisses me on the lips like we're old friends. In the space of pouring me a glass of wine, he introduces me to about a dozen guys. Half of them are already out of it. One immediately offers me an e. I turn it down but accept a joint. Dope relaxes me. It also makes me more distant, less easy to get close to. And this is skunk, which always makes me feel like there's a thick, dark green forest growing around my thought processes and leaves my clothes smelling like stale brussel sprouts left over from Christmas dinner.

An hour drifts by. I dance a little. I like to dance. Guys hit on me but when you're dancing it's easy to avoid them without giving offence. Let them think I'm loved up and into the music. More people arrive. The lager's run out but there are still wine boxes and spirits have started emerging. I fill a big glass with vodka, coke and ice, then wander outside.

On a moonlight night, like tonight, you can see the sea from the garden. There's a fresh breeze and my head no longer feels so cooked.

'Allison!' There's a gaggle of people from my year in an unlit corner by the fence that separates the garden from The Common. They're watching Tom Piper have a conversation with an over-sized gnome. This is what passes for humour in my circle. Tom got popular playing the class clown at the beginning of sixth form (we were all in single sex schools before that) but his act is getting pretty old. Seeing me, he snaps out of it.

'Hey, Allison! Where's Mark?'

'In Ibiza, with Helen Kent.'

'She's a gold-digger. It won't last. He'll come back to you, hon.'

'Actually, I dumped him, Tom.'

Jo Ford starts to bitch about Helen, but this is only because Pete Robben dumped her for Helen when she arrived in the lower sixth and Jo has never forgiven her, even though the blame clearly lies with Pete.

'I like Helen,' I lie. 'She seems to be good for Mark.'

'You're always so balanced,' Phil Jones says. 'Even though Helen was always trying to get off with Mark when you were going out with him.'

'If she was, I didn't notice.' Though Mark probably did. He has better romance radar than me, sussed that Phil and Tom were playing hide the banana long before either of them came out.

'Oh Christ,' Jo says. 'Look who's here!'

Night is falling fast but that has nothing to do with the shadow that seems to fall across my friends. I recognise one of the two people who have just come through the French doors: Huw Evans, who was in the year above us. I recall there was a story about him when I came back at Easter, but can't remember what it was. I'm more interested in hearing the story of the guy who's with Huw. He's stick thin with a mop of curly, jet black hair and sunken eyes.

'Who's that with Huw?' I ask Jo.

'Aidan Kinsale.'

'He's cute. I don't remember him from Calday.'

'No, he went to a public school.'

They're coming over. Aidan, with his rock star hair and gypsy eyes, has given a face to a long held but very blurred fantasy.

'You know what happened with them, don't you?' Jo asks.

Before I can answer, there's a loud 'wa-hey!' from the French doors and we watch half a dozen of Dom Pritchard's mates carrying their host above their heads. They seem intent on throwing him over the fence into The Common. Zoe follows them out, yelling that they'd better not injure him or the party will be over. The rugby players revise their plans, hurling Dom into a flower bed. Amidst this mayhem, I still have my eye on Aidan Kinsale, and so does Zoe. I watch as she goes over and kisses him on the cheek, gives him a little hug. Has she got in there first? I decide to chance it, say 'hello'. Zoe invited me, and I haven't spoken to her since we arrived.

'What happened there?' I ask Zoe, who's standing between Aidan and Huw. 'Did they have something against Dom?'

'Search me. It's what happens when you give cocaine to children.'

I look at Aidan. He really is gorgeous — out of my league, and Zoe's.

'Hi,' I say, fed up of waiting for her to introduce us.

'Sorry,' Zoe says. 'Allison, this is Aidan, an old friend.'

I smile at Aidan and nod at Huw, who gives me a sheepish, gormless grin. Maybe he and Aidan are a couple, I think. Maybe that's what Jo was hinting about a minute ago. There seems to be an invisible string binding them together. Zoe looks at the way I'm looking at Aidan and something passes between us. She grabs Huw's arm. 'Aidan, I think you and Allison will find you have a lot in common. Huw, there's someone I want you to meet.'

Aidan says nothing and I search for something to say, knowing that whatever comes out of my mouth at the moment is going to sound silly and girly. 'So shall we try and play the game, work out what it is that Zoe thinks we have in common?'

He doesn't object, so I plough in. 'Do you read a lot?'

I read somewhere that during the course of a day women talk, on average, three times more than men. With me and Aidan, it's more like ten to one. We play favourite authors, though it rapidly becomes apparent that Aidan's more of an indie comics guy. We bond over a couple of bands. Aidan has a sexy half-smile, one that crinkles around the corners of his lips but doesn't dance across his gentle eyes. I discover that he lives in Birkenhead, ten miles away.

'How do you know Zoe?'

'We used to go out, when she was in Lower Sixth. I was at school with her brother.'

'Really?' *She kept you quiet,* I'm thinking.

'Yeah, on and off until she started university.'

'I see.' I see a lot. This explains Zoe's seeming inability to form lasting relationships, her legendary propensity for one night stands that stop short of full sex. She had a secret boyfriend in Birkenhead.

'Didn't you go to uni?'

'Yeah. Liverpool. I dropped out though.'

'Oh.'

'I'll probably go back one day. I like studying. It was just...'

His voice trails off and I decide not to ask "why" or say anything that sounds like an interrogation. I don't want this one to get away, even if he is one of Zoe's cast-offs.

Aidan doesn't have a drink, I notice.

'Shall we get another drink?'

He shakes his head. 'It's like a scrum in there. I've got a spliff if you want to share one.'

'OK. Fancy a go on the swings?'

At the far end of the garden, away from the party, are a set of double swings with peeling green paint, from Dom and Zoe's childhood. We swing gently, passing the spliff, enjoying each other's company without saying much. The joint's even stronger than the last one, harsh on the throat. I offer Aidan my drink to help him wash it down. He takes one sip and spits it out.

'I don't drink alcohol.'

'Why not?'

'I like to stay in control.'

'Very admirable,' I say, though I don't know how his sobriety squares with the joint we're sharing. There goes my plan to get Aidan drunk and seduce him. Dope makes me randy, but doesn't have that effect on guys. They need booze to loosen their inhibitions. I'm not drunk. I'm floating. Within the warm, throbbing membrane that is my brain, my mind feels ultra clear. I like Aidan. I like that he's a man of a few words. I want him.

'Do you want to go inside?' I say. He shakes his head.

'I prefer it out here.'

I should add, 'I meant upstairs,' but girls don't say that kind of thing. At least, I don't. And Zoe's lot are pretty wild. The bedrooms are probably all occupied. I can hear a rustle in the darkness that may easily be a couple fucking. There's another huge cheer. Somebody else is being carried out of the party, this time to the pond. Aidan winces.

44

'Do you want to go to mine?' I say. 'I live across The Common. It's just me at the moment. My mum's in Spain.'

'I can't leave Huw,' he says. 'I'm staying at his.'

Should I be hearing warning bells? Part of me admires his loyalty, his diffidence. Most blokes would dump their friends at the first hint of a casual fuck.

'We can come back later.' Does this sound like begging?

'OK,' he says.

It's a balmy evening. People are coming and going and nobody pays any attention as we head out of the side gate onto the street and into The Common. I start to head uphill, hoping we'll have enough conversation for the fifteen minute walk. I can already sense that Aidan's getting cold feet.

'Wait,' he says.

'What?'

'Let's walk on the beach. I like the beach at night.'

'Me too.'

This isn't what I had in mind but maybe it's a better idea than rushing him into bed. Good things are worth waiting for, I persuade myself, and Aidan doesn't seem like the sort of bloke who can be rushed into anything. We stumble over stubble and he takes my arm to hold me steady. My hand slips into his and stays there. A moon, nearly full, slips from behind the clouds. At the bottom of The Common, we cross a road, go down a lane, and we have the whole beach to ourselves. The sea is far away.

'What's that island over there?' Aidan asks.

'Hilbre. You can walk over there at low tide. I've done it a couple of times.'

'Shall we?' His tone is more playful than serious, but I answer seriously.

'You don't start from here. And there are patches of quicksand. It's not safe in the dark.'

'Call this dark?'

We walk along the beach, but not for long. After a while, we sit on a rock, look at the moon, listen to the distant sea, our arms around each other. The kiss, when it comes, feels natural. There's another. And another. His kisses are soft, moist, smokey. He doesn't try to feel me up. Nor does he suggest that we lie on the tufty grass at the edge of the sand. After a while, he pulls away.

'We ought to go back,' he says.

I stop myself from asking 'why?' He's older than me, and more sober, so I stand up as he does and we walk back up to Zoe's, holding hands. I mean to suggest again that he could stay at mine tonight but haven't worked up the nerve yet. Don't rush a good thing, I keep warning myself. Aidan stops holding my hand and gets out another spliff. I don't know why he needs it when we're having such a good time already. Without a drink to wash it down, the smoke is acrid and brittle, making me splutter. I hardly have time to pass it back before I'm gagging. Then I'm puking up on the sand. Not a full upchuck, but a pint or so of rum and coke mixed with party pizza — a melange fully illuminated by the romantic moonlight.

Aidan pulls a handkerchief from the front right pocket of his jeans. An old-fashioned, white linen hanky. I didn't know anyone still used them any more. I wipe my mouth. My clothes are OK. All of the mess is on the sand. I'm mortified. I haven't thrown up at a party since I was fifteen.

'Are you OK?'

'Fine. It went down the wrong way. I suddenly feel very sober though. And embarrassed.'

46

'Don't be.' He smiles. 'You seem like one of those people who hardly ever lets go.'

'There's some truth in that.' I pause, waiting to hear some more of his insights into me, but that's all I'm getting. So I ask about him.

'Why did you drop out?'

He doesn't answer at first. I'm about to say something, anything else, when he tells me.

'I was in hospital for six months.'

'What happened?' He doesn't answer and I realise that it was a mental thing, so try to make it easy for him. 'Depression?'

I know about depression, kind of. My mum claims to suffer from it and self-medicates with alcohol, except when she's on the wagon.

'Not exactly. A kind of breakdown. It's complicated. Huw and I were...'

His mobile rings and he answers it at once.

'Yeah, sorry. I'm on the beach. I'll be five minutes at most. Sorry. Right.'

He puts the phone away. 'My lift's waiting for me.'

It's only midnight. I feel closer to him after he told me about the breakdown and I want to invite him to stay at mine. But he's just watched me puke up and he has white linen hankies that his mum has ironed. And he has to leave a party at midnight when he's twenty-one years old.

'Am I going to see you again?' I ask.

He doesn't look at me as he replies. 'When you get back to the party, they'll talk about me and Huw. You won't want to see me after you've heard.'

That's such a weird thing to say that I don't take it in.

'Why don't you give me your number?' I say, as we walk

up the hill. 'Then I can decide.'

'I don't have a pen.'

Neither do I. I tell Aidan my mum's surname and the road
we live on, ask him to call me. The hospital thing and the last
cryptic exchange has unnerved me a little. He's a little distant.
So what? I tell myself. I can be a little distant myself. Of
course, if you meet your ideal boyfriend, there has to be a
price to pay, a hurdle or two to leap. As we turn onto Zoe's
street, I ask for his email address even though I know I'll forget
it in minutes.

Huw's dad is waiting, engine running. Aidan gets in the
back of the car without kissing me, without saying goodnight.
Huw stares straight ahead. They drive off and I go back into
the party, where dance music has been replaced by heavy
metal. Or maybe it's thrash metal. I'm not very good on the
subgenres of cock-rock. I hurry upstairs where the bathroom,
miracle of miracles, is free, and has a lock that works. I wash
my mouth out and — gross, I know — steal somebody's
electric toothbrush to get the vomit taste off my teeth. I
borrow some of Zoe's mascara to freshen up and am almost
done when there's a fierce pounding on the door. I open it
and one of the rugby player types barges past me, then
begins puking into the toilet bowl.

The kitchen is crowded and drink is at a premium. I pour
myself a mug of tap water and, not seeing anyone I want to
talk to, slide back out into the garden. Zoe's still there, with
the gang from our year. I'm about to join them when I realise
that they're talking about Aidan.

'I couldn't live with what Aidan did.' Phil.

'People can live with anything.' Jo.

'It was as much Huw's fault, egging him on.' Tom.

'He's not the same, Huw, since it happened.' Jo.

'I heard he's got religion.' Phil.

'Bit late for that.' Jo.

'At least he's going back to uni,' Zoe says. 'Aidan just sits in his room all day, that's what his mum told me.'

'How come you spoke to Aidan's mum?' Jo asks.

'They're old family friends,' Zoe says, giving nothing away.

'Maybe Allison figures she can cure him,' Jo says.

'Did I hear my name being taken in vain?' I interrupt, before anyone notices me eavesdropping. It's never good to overhear conversations about yourself. They tell you that in all the manuals and pre-twentieth century novels. Tom turns to Zoe.

'Did anyone tell Allison about Aidan?'

'I was going to,' Zoe says, addressing her reply to me. 'But I thought he might tell you himself and I didn't want you to, you know, prejudge him.'

'Because he had a breakdown?'

'Is that what he called it?' Phil sniggers. 'The guy's a walking car crash.'

'Fuck off, Phil,' Zoe says.

'What?' Phil, drunk, can't see what the problem is with his humour.

'I'm trying to tell Allison something serious. Fuck off and roll us a spliff. She'll need one afterwards.'

It's the last thing I need, but Phil and Tom fade away, followed by Jo. Zoe explains.

'It's to do with what caused the breakdown,' she says. 'I used to go out with Aidan, on and off, I don't know if he told you. We split up when he went to uni.'

'He told me,' I say. 'But there was something else he wouldn't tell me. He said I'd find out as soon as I got back.'

Zoe's words come out in a rush. 'Last summer, after Aidan

passed his test, he and Huw drove around a lot. They were always great mates and I could never understand why they got on so well, but anyway... they started playing this game. I'm surprised you didn't hear about it.'

Something about a car crash starts coming back to me. Playing chicken.

'They would drive as close as they could to the car in front, so close that, if the car in front braked at all, the bumpers would meet. The idea was to freak the car in front out. Since they couldn't stop, they'd have to swerve off the road, or drive so fast they outpaced Aidan and Huw.'

I say nothing. This dumb story is only heading in one direction.

'They did it for a few weeks before it went wrong. An elderly couple drove off the road, into a tree. He broke his neck, died instantly. She was saved by the airbag but broke her spine. Paralysed from the waist down.'

'Shit.' Led Zeppelin come on. Nearby, a woman opens a bedroom window, yells for somebody to turn the music down. No-one does.

'Aidan had a breakdown afterwards. He got off lightly in court. Suspended sentence for dangerous driving. Banned for ten years.'

'And Huw?'

'He wasn't prosecuted. His parents paid for a good lawyer who advised him not to say anything about anything to anyone. He used to go and see Aidan every week in hospital. Did Aidan tell you any of this?'

I shake my head. 'He said I'd find out and afterwards and then I wouldn't want to see him again.'

'And do you?'

'I don't know.' I hesitate. I'm freaked out, but want to say something nice to Zoe, who clearly cares about Aidan. 'He talked about you. He seems very fond of you.'

'I love Aidan, but more like family, you know? He's very naive in some ways. With the car crash, I doubt it ever occurred to him that anybody could get hurt.'

I find myself thinking aloud. 'You make him sound like a dead loss.'

'I just want you to know what you're getting into if you go out with him. He needs to heal. You'd be really good for him, Allison. He's a fantastic guy when you get to know him.'

She's still a little in love with Aidan, I see, but I can't blame her for that. I like that she's looking out for him. Funny how I like Zoe much more since we left school, since her dad tried to rape me.

'You enjoy a rescue mission. Mark was such a fuck-up before he went out with you. As soon as you dumped him he landed Miss Junior High!'

I laugh. Do I like a rescue mission? What does that make me, if I'm drawn to fucked-up guys? Mark wasn't all that fucked-up. He was lonely and angry, like half the people at this party.

'Will you see Aidan again?'

'That's up to him. I gave him my number. If he can't remember it, he can always get it off you.'

The boys return with the joint. I sidle off before it comes to me. I take the long way home, even though it's a moonlit night and I'd be home in half the time if I walked across The Common. There are nutters in the world, and you don't put yourself at risk unless you really, really have to. I think about Aidan and whether I could accept what he did — taking one life and ruining another. I wonder whether he can accept himself. I doubt that he'll call, but what if he does? We made a connection. Good people do bad things. You have to cut everyone a break from time to time if you're going to get by in this world. Also, I think he's gorgeous.

On the debit side, there's something bleak about him. I know that empty look. I've felt like that myself sometimes, like, when you get to basics, nothing mean anything. That emptiness is what allowed him and Huw to drive like devils. And I can see how easily that nullity, that despair, could suck me in. It's not my job to rescue him, I decide. It's his job to rescue himself. If he can do that, then I'll go out with him.

SEPTEMBER

Summer ends abruptly, three weeks before the start of term. My job ends too. I was covering for holiday leave, but everyone's back. So are Mark and Helen, with their Ibiza tans. I meet them for a drink in the Black Horse.

'Aren't you going off somewhere?' Mark asks.

'Maybe,' I say. 'It's complicated.'

'Have you met someone?' Helen asks, for I never get Mark on his own these days. After a wobble earlier in the year, they have become that obnoxious thing, the perfect, prematurely middle-aged couple. Both got their grades and are following me to Nottingham next month. Hip hip hooray.

'Sort of,' I say, 'but I'm not sure he's the Ibiza type.' And I'm not sure that I am. In my gang, such as it is, I was always the last one to do everything, smoke weed, take e, lose my virginity, and I still haven't been on a holiday abroad with my mates, never mind with a boyfriend. Mark and I did take a tent to the Lake District once, but I haven't left the UK since Mum and Dad took me to France when I was thirteen. Whereas half my year at uni have been to Africa or Thailand.

Sensing my discomfort, Mark switches the conversation to Nottingham. I go on to autopilot, thinking about what I'll say in my email to Aidan when I get home. He got my email address off Zoe and started writing to me every day. Sometimes there are several emails waiting when I get back from work. This has been going on since the party but I haven't met him since then. He never phones, either. When I call him, the awkward silences make me understand why.

I don't want to push it. He's been through a lot. Accident. Hospital. Everyone looking at him weirdly. I don't tell Mark and Helen that I'm into him. That might jinx our chances and Aidan's jinxed enough already.

'And where are you living this year?' Helen asks me.

'A house in Lenton.'

'Who with?'

'My friend Vic and three other people.'

None of whom I really know, which would sound sad, only Helen isn't all that interested so doesn't interrogate me over who the others might be. Vic has sorted out a bloke to replace Paul. He will have the inferior first floor room, leaving me with the attic one, which is what I wanted.

'I'd better get off,' I say. 'I've got my driving test tomorrow.'

This throws them a little. I leave in a hail of 'good luck's without revealing that my test is not until three in the afternoon and I have no intention of going to bed early.

There's an email from Aidan waiting when I get home. He writes surreal emails with jokes and poems in which one or the other of us is a character (but never the two of us together). I told him about the driving test then immediately regretted it, because he has a ten year ban. But I wanted him to know that, if I passed, I'd be able to drive over and see him. At the end of the email, he wishes me luck and says 'be good to see you again'. Where he lives, it's a train and a bus and a long walk, a ninety minute journey, but it would take less than half an hour in a car.

There's loads riding on the test. My dad, guilty about Christmas, has promised to buy me a car if I pass, and to pay the first year's insurance. We hardly communicate, but he's been paying for two lessons a week all summer, which adds up. My instructor says I have a fifty-fifty chance. My mum hardly ever takes me out (she's a nervous driver) but says I can use her car if I pass. I could go and see Aidan tomorrow.

Why didn't I learn when all my friends did? It has something to do with my seventeenth birthday coming so late in August. I wanted to concentrate on school and I didn't want to ask Dad for anything. I had to wait until he offered.

The test flies by. Three point turn. Emergency stop. I'm nearly back at the test centre, my head reeling with the thought that I might have done it, when, at the junction before the test centre, the examiner gives an instruction that confuses me.

'Follow the road as the signs indicate.'

I'm so busy working out what the signs say and whether there's a twist to his directions that I've missed, I fail to notice the lights have changed. The examiner points this out, loudly and nervously. Back at the centre, I know I've failed and hardly take in his words. This is the first time I've failed anything. My love life, I'm sure, has also failed.

My instructor says she'll get me a cancellation before I return to uni. If I leave it until Christmas, the nights will be short and I'll have forgotten most of what I learnt this summer. I phone Aidan to tell him the bad news.

'...so I can't drive over, not while I'm home this time anyway.'

'Why don't I come and see you?' he says, to my surprise. Easy as that.

I meet him at the station. He's on time, and as attractive as I remember, though it's not the weather for the junk shop tweed overcoat he's wearing. We go for a walk through town and end up on the beach again. Aidan keeps his hands in his coat pockets. I think of hooking my arm through his but that might be too soppy. Aidan walks fast on the windy beach. At times I struggle to keep up. I remind him about Hilbre Island, over on our right, bird watchers' paradise. The night we met, he claimed not to have heard of it, but now I know he comes to West Kirby a lot, so that can't be true. I'm only starting to get used to his sense of humour.

'Next time, maybe we can walk there.'

'Why not today?'

'You need to go out at low tide and stay there for five hours before you can walk back again. We'd need to plan it.'

'How long does it take?'

'A couple of hours. Maybe a little less.'

I am about to say that there's a shorter route from Red Rocks in Hoylake but Aidan has a kind of gleam in his eye and I sense that, if there is a more dangerous route, he'd take it.

'We could go tomorrow, if you stayed over.'

'Do you want to? Would your mum mind?'

'I don't think she'd even notice.'

Tired from our beach walk, we get the bus up the hill. I ask him about his friendship with Huw. This is the nearest I'll get to asking him about the accident. Unless he brings it up himself.

'Huw's... Huw. I've known him since Infants. He used to live in Birkenhead.'

'How is he?'

'Dunno. I've not seen him much lately.'

'We could go round to his later if you want.'

Aidan doesn't respond to this and I'm not keen, though visiting Huw would be a way of legitimising Aidan's putative position as my boyfriend.

'Someone said Huw's going back to uni next month.'

'Yeah. He'll be a second year, like you.'

'Have you thought about going back?'

Silence.

'You're not ready.'

'Maybe. I don't...' Long pause. 'Everybody knows.'

I don't know how to respond to this, so I kiss him. He kisses me back, a long, soft kiss. We miss our stop and have to walk back to mine along the side of The Common. Once we're home, I take him straight up to my room.

I don't want Aidan to think I'm a slut but there's only an hour before Mum gets back from work and I want to have sex with him. I want to have sex while I'm sober. He doesn't resist. We undress ourselves and he doesn't have a condom so I have to find a packet that's been at the back of a drawer since Christmas. We fumble around with the curtains closed. I have to help him inside. It's nice, but it's over almost before it's begun. My first time with a virgin. What's nicer is after-wards, holding him, flesh on flesh.

Later, after Mum has gone to bed and we've watched a silly horror movie, we do it again. And this time it's better, better than the three times I've done it before, better than good. It's the intimacy that amazes me, the having him inside me and the smell of him all over me and the way he's so gentle and loving. At three in the morning he goes back to the spare room and I wonder what I'll do in the morning after Mum's gone to work. How will I explain to Aidan that I don't have any more condoms? There were only two left in the packet because I used one with Mark at Christmas. But I won't need to explain. He'll assume I've been doing it for years, like most of my mates. Only I'm not like most of my mates. And neither is he.

I wake at nine, early for me, early enough for us to go for our walk to Hilbre. When I take Aidan a mug of tea in bed, he's gone. No note, nothing.

✠

What sort of guy disappears in the middle of the night? Five nights later, I go for a drink with Mark. Aidan hasn't answered my emails since he left. I have to tell someone, and Mark knows me better than anyone. I need his advice.

'I've been seeing this guy called Aidan Kinsale. Do you know him?'

Mark shakes his head. That was easy. I relax. I'm killing two birds with one stone: Mark will tell Helen I've got a boyfriend and she'll decide it's safe for him to see me alone. I tell Mark a bit about Aidan, skirting over the car crash stuff.

'I'm not sure if we're going out, as such. But we're friends.'

'Helen says men and women can't be friends. There's always a sexual element. That's why she doesn't like me seeing you alone.'

'Does that mean I can expect her to walk through the door any minute?'

He laughs awkwardly, indicating that Helen knows where he is. I join in, acknowledging that neither of us would put it past her to turn up. This lends some urgency to our conversation.

'Have you slept with him?' Mark asks.

I glare at him. He has no right to ask me this question. Not in public. Not at all.

'Would you be jealous if I had?'

Before Mark can answer this, Helen arrives, wearing a bustier that reveals her Ibiza tan to boy-stunning advantage. I blush to think how stupid my last question was. Mark only wanted to know how close I'd let myself get to Aidan before he offered me his advice. He's getting grade A sex from the sexy sexpert who's just sat down and has no reason to be jealous of anybody.

It's my round. When I return, Helen asks me about the driving test. I explain that I'm retaking it the day before I go back to uni, which means I'm living in West Kirby until the last possible moment, which wasn't in my plans. We're about to leave when Helen says, apropos of nothing, 'Did you two hear about Huw? You were at school with him, right?'

'Huw?' Mark says.

'Used to go to Calday. He was in that horrible accident, where...'

'We know. What about him?'

'He died in a car crash, last Monday. The funeral was today.'

I freeze. My chin quivers, thinking of Aidan, but Helen doesn't notice.

'Do you know how it happened?' Mark asks.

'He was in the car alone, that's all I know, ran into a tree.'

'Lost control or...?'

Helen shrugs. 'I never liked him much. He tried to get off with me at a party when I was in Year Eleven. Arrogant tosser. Hands all over the place. But you wouldn't wish that on anyone.'

At home, I write Aidan an email offering my condolences with an unspoken question: when did he find out? Was there a text in the middle of the night? I get a polite email back, perfectly spelt and punctuated, unlike his other emails.

I couldn't sleep, he says. *I don't know if it was because of what happened between us or because I sensed what Huw had done. I had to go home as soon as it was light. I waited at the station for an hour before the first train came.* He invites me to visit him in Birkenhead. *You're all I have now.* I reply at once, before I take these last words in, saying I'll go. Then I begin to worry. His oldest and best friend has just died. I'm getting in too deep, too fast.

✠

Next day, I ring Zoe. She's surprised I'm still around. I explain about the driving test. She tells me about the funeral.

'Not many people were there. It was horrible. Everyone crying. The vicar gave this icky talk about guilt and God's forgiveness.'

'How did Aidan take it?'

'Aidan wasn't there. I'm not sure if that was his choice. Maybe Huw's parents didn't want him there. Or perhaps Aidan couldn't face it. I don't suppose you've heard from him since my party?'

'Actually... I've seen him once.'

'That's good. I mean, I'm surprised, but it's good. Does he talk to you? Because, when we were going out, I did 90% of the talking. Which, at first, I thought was cool, a guy who listens. But then I began to worry that he didn't know how to communicate, didn't know how to read his own thoughts, never mind anyone else's. He and Huw seemed ascloseasthis but, whenever I was with the two of them, they never really talked to each other, not about anything. A couple of words here, a glance there, that was all they had to communicate.'

'I do most of the talking,' I said, then ask the question that's been on my mind since the night I met Aidan. 'Do you know whose idea it was, the chicken game with cars?'

'Aidan was driving, but the idea... it sounds more like Huw to me.'

'Do you think Huw meant to kill himself?'

'I don't know. The whisper was that he'd had a lot to drink.'

'At least Aidan doesn't drink,' I say.

'He used to,' Zoe tells me. 'He used to take anything and everything.'

✠

Aidan's mum collects me from the station. Even though Aidan's not with her, we recognise each other at once. I am the only skinny nineteen year-old in sight, while she's pretty much the same age as my mum, but better preserved. She has an immaculately made up version of Aidan's mouth, Aidan's nose. Mrs Kinsale doesn't explain her son's absence. After we get into her smart Alfa Romeo, she launches into a series of warning signs.

'It's great that he's met someone. Aidan says that you're a very caring person, very clever, too. Of course, I can tell what he sees in you.'

I don't recognise myself from this description. Maybe mothers have a special way of viewing their son's world. Linda Kinsale tells me that Huw's death has hit Aidan hard. He's been behaving strangely. Off his meds. Both families thought it best he didn't attend the funeral. She asks how much I know about 'the accident'.

'I was at university when it happened. All I heard was that they were playing a dare game and it went wrong. Aidan doesn't talk about it.'

'He's the same with me. Those two boys, when they were together, they always created their own little world. I don't think either of them appreciated the risks. His father...'

We pull into the driveway of a modern, detached house with a substantial garden at the front. She doesn't finish the sentence. Aidan, to my mind, belongs in a Gothic pile, or at least an attic room like the one I'm about to have, with a skylight and wooden floorboards. Instead, he inhabits a concrete prefab. I walk over the fitted pastel carpets, look politely at the framed prints of 'modern' paintings that decorate every wall.

'Aidan!' Linda calls. 'Allison's here.' No reply. 'He must be in his room.'

'Would you show me where it is?'

Linda guides me upstairs into a wide, airy hallway, then up a narrow, winding stairwell into the converted loft. She knocks on the door but opens it without waiting for an answer.

'Aid, Allison's here.'

The room is stuffy. Body odours mixed with stale air suffused with skunk. Linda doesn't comment on this. Aidan's in bed, asleep. His mum opens the window. I look around, wondering what I'm doing here. It's like a palace, this room. Large bed, widescreen TV and a computer with a screen twice the size of mine. Two games consoles. Comic book artwork on the wall, some of it signed originals, in frames. A stack of CDs and DVDs several feet high. A stereo that's bigger than Mark's, and he's into his music, whereas Aidan is pushed to name a band he half likes.

The carpet is thick pile, purple. The bright midday light reveals beer stains and hash burns. There are no bookshelves, only comics in purpose-built boxes and a stack of graphic novels beneath the metal bed base. Aidan rubs his eyes.

'I'll make some coffee,' Linda says. 'How do you take it?'

'Black. Strong.'

'I think that's what he needs, too.'

She closes the door behind her. Aidan gets up. I've never seen him naked before. Not properly. He's even thinner than I thought, his bony chest unhealthily pale but for grey-pink, inverted nipples. His pubic hair is a shock of black barbed wire inside which his penis nestles like a dormouse. He blinks at me, says 'shower', then disappears into an adjacent room. He has his own, en-suite bathroom. He is a spoilt man-child and I don't know why I am taking him under my wing.

When Linda returns with the coffee, Aidan is still in the shower. She points to a shelf by the main window.

'He'll be better if he takes those.'

His meds. Three separate bottles.

'He doesn't always?'

'You know what he's like.'

I don't. Not really. Not at all.

'You started to say something about his father earlier,' I say. 'Aidan never mentions him.'

'He left, when Aidan was five. He's abroad now. There's been no contact for ten years or so. My second husband, Aidan's stepfather, adopted him. But they're not close. The only person to get close was Huw.'

There's a younger brother and sister, I recall. Half brother and sister. They must be at school. She goes on.

'You're the first girl he's ever invited back here, Allison. He must think an awful lot of you'.

She smiles weakly, then leaves.

I listen to the shower. Huw replaced Aidan's dad and now I am to replace Huw. If I were to turn and run now, nobody would blame me afterwards.

I drink some of my coffee. Espresso, rocket fuel. I can do this, I think, as the caffeine hits. I can take this on. Me and Aidan against the world.

For I need someone to love. And so does he. We can be everything to each other. I can take him out of this sterile, cosy hideaway and bring him to Nottingham. I'll cure him and he'll cure me.

The bathroom door opens. Aidan's body is lithe and wet, glistening in the silver sun.

'Sorry I kept you waiting,' he says.

SOPHOMORES

Sophomore is the word for a second year university student. It's derived from *Sophism* which means *false argument* or *to lie*. I like to know where words come from. This one goes back to a Greek word for a teacher of philosophy. Some second years think they're sophisticated: subtle, complex, worldly. They're lying to themselves.

I put this in an email to Aidan and he comes back with a word that isn't in my dictionary: *sophomoric*. This means *behaviour typical of a sophomore: immature, superficial, crude or inflated in manner.* I decide to avoid being all of these things. I will work hard. I will write for the university newspaper, in case I decide to pursue journalism after I graduate. I will be sociable but slightly aloof from the other people in my house.

It's Freshers' Week, only this year they've turned it into Freshers' Fortnight, with 'welcome back' events for second years in the second week. My room is in the attic. I have a view of the road below, and a dormer window through which I can see the stars. My room is directly above Steve, the last minute substitute for Paul. He's doing Electronics.

We've hardly spoken to so far. I know he's straight. His bed frame is noisy and some of his partners are particularly loud. Freshers' week is made for guys like Steve, who come on all sophisticated to impressionable first year girls. Last night, at midnight, I went down to the toilet and heard a girl with a Sloane accent telling him loudly and enthusiastically how grateful she was to him for deflowering her. Yuck.

Maybe he was doing her a favour, I think as I get off the train in West Kirby on Friday afternoon. Maybe getting it over with is what your first week at uni is all about. I should have done that myself rather than waiting until Christmas to seduce my ex-boyfriend. At nineteen, I shouldn't be able to count the number of times I've had sex on the fingers of one hand. I shouldn't be able to count them, full stop.

Last year, I never went home at weekends during term time, but then I didn't have a boyfriend in Birkenhead. Or a car to pick up. I passed my test ten days ago and Dad has promised me my own Mini.

I spend an evening with Mum and collect the car in the morning. It's pillar box red. I'd like to have a target painted on the roof but Dad tells me this would be expensive, and ostentatious.

'Don't let one of your mates do it. They'll wreck the thing. A car like this holds its value if you look after it.'

'When are we going to meet this boyfriend of yours?' Ingrid asks.

'You may have to wait until the wedding,' I say, which throws her.

I drive over to Birkenhead, where my lover's mother gives me tea and cake and marvels at the hundred mile journey I am about to make.

'You're fearless, Allison,' she says, implying that my taking

66

on her son is part of that fearlessness. Then she tells me that Aidan won't be joining us for a while as he hasn't left his room for two days. I pretend to laugh this off.

'He's been sleeping a lot more since Huw died,' she says. 'Leave him to me.'

Aidan is fast out in his large, metallic bed. When I open the blinds, he doesn't stir. I have a shower, then get into bed next to him. The pills that were on the window ledge last time I came are now by the bed. I wonder how many anti-depressants he's on but don't know which is which. There's only one pill I know the name of and Aidan doesn't take it. I, on the other hand, am anxious to justify its daily imposition. But I can't seduce Aidan unless he opens his eyes.

Oh. I can.

'That was exciting,' I tell Aidan afterwards, but he's gone back to sleep. I'm disappointed. It's not that I'm looking for someone like Steve, who's driven by his dick, and gives me lascivious looks all the time (I expect he does the same to Vic and Tessa, too, but I'm home more). It's just that I worry Aidan doesn't fancy me as much as I'd like him to. I'm worried that he doesn't talk to me.

I shouldn't be so self-obsessed. He's depressed because his best friend killed himself last month. He's allowed to fall asleep after sex. Men do that.

I read a couple of the comics on his desk, silly tales about superheroes whose powers alienate them from the people they have vowed to protect. I put on one of Aidan's Kraut-rock LPs. That's right, a vinyl record. He pays a fortune for them on eBay. He says the scratches and static crackle make them sound more authentic.

When it starts to get dark, his mum knocks on the door and invites me to eat with the rest of the family.

'We do appreciate you trying so hard, Allison,' step-dad Keith says, over lasagne and Chianti.

Half-sister Anna gives me a suspicious look that tells me she suspects what I've been up to with her brother and does not approve. At thirteen, I'd probably feel the same way. When I accept a second glass of wine, Anna asks me if I'm driving home later. I take a deep gulp before breaking the awkward silence that follows.

'I told my mum I was staying here tonight. I want to be here when Aidan wakes up even if, you know, it's four in the morning.'

'Where will you sleep?'

'In his bed, of course,' I say.

Anna gives her mum a shocked look. She's revived the thirteen year old bitch in me. Keith raises an eyebrow in what would probably become a wink if he didn't think better of it and start talking about his own university days instead. I nod enthusiastically when he goes on about seeing 'The Floyd' though I'm not certain what or who he's talking about. When dinner's over, I help Anna clear the table.

'Can't you take him to Nottingham?' Anna hisses as we load the dishwasher. 'It's like living in a psychiatric ward, having him here. These are meant to be my years in the granny flat before granny moves in. Not his.'

'I'm sorry. He's not my responsibility.'

'I didn't say he was. It's just, you're strong. I'll bet you could shake him out of it.'

'I'm trying, believe me. I do care about him, a lot.'

'I don't. And Dad only pretends to.'

Watching TV with them later, the conversation is forced, mundane. Everyone's life is on hold, waiting for Aidan. I don't know what I'm doing here.

'I'm going up to my night vigil,' I announce when the late film starts.

I find Aidan awake, dressed and at his computer.

'I thought I'd dreamt you coming,' he says.

'You say the most romantic things.'

'Did we... earlier?'

'You had a wet dream, yeah.'

He kisses me. His hair is moist from the shower. He shows me a site he likes and we look at it together. We start to play, making up names for each other. Imaginary animals take imaginary drugs that combine sexual ecstasy with profound self-perception. Later, when everyone's gone to bed, Aidan goes downstairs and eats cereal and toast with huge mugs of builders' tea.

We watch a science fiction DVD. Aidan devours several joints, with only a little assistance from me. We cuddle, but he shows no desire to go back to bed for an encore. At four in the morning, I fall asleep. When I wake, I'm in bed, in my underwear. Aidan is dead to the world, even harder to rouse than he was yesterday. I shower and go downstairs. The house is empty but for him.

While the family are at church, I write Aidan a note, asking him to visit me. It wouldn't be difficult. His mum'd drive him to Lime St Station. I'd collect him in Nottingham. In the note, I tell him I'm worried that he never sees daylight, sleeps twelve hours or more a day. I want to finish it 'I love you', but we haven't used these words and they seem to be too much of a hostage to fortune. Only what am I doing here if I don't love him?

Some people never use the word 'love'. Love is like religion, rationally impossible but easy to subscribe to if you find yourself blessed with faith. But people's feelings for each other shouldn't be a matter of belief. I haven't believed in God for five years, but I'm not so sure about love. I know what I want love to be, like a rollercoaster, crushing everything in its path, possessing me utterly. But not everyone can feel that. Maybe my emotions are always going to be minor key piano pieces, rather than loud power chords on an electric guitar. What I feel for Aidan is stronger than what I felt for Mark. Or is it just different? If I made an Aidan pie chart it would show forty percent infatuation, fifty percent lust, and ten percent my appetite for taking risks.

I brew some coffee then drive to Nottingham, taking note of the speed cameras my dad warned me about yesterday. When I get back, the other four are making a roast chicken dinner and invite me to join them. We agreed not to cook together, so I'm happily surprised.

I make gravy from a packet. Steve is all smiles. The others tease him about the girl he brought home last night. Vic says she can use some tips on pick-up techniques. Steve offers to set up a threesome, which makes Vic blush. I've never seen her blush before. Did she consider his offer, if only for a moment?

'Visiting your boyfriend?' Steve asks, as he begins to carve.

'That's right,' I reply. 'We spent all weekend in bed.'

NEW
AGE

When he discovered that both Vic and I had our birthdays just before we moved in, Steve suggested we have a house party. He assumed I was twenty, like Vic, and I didn't correct him. I never looked like the youngest person in my year, but I always was. Mark used to tease me about my birth sign. *Virgo by name, virgo by nature,* though he hasn't done this since he slept with me.

I told Steve I wasn't bothered about a party, pretended I'd had one at home during vacation. The other three over-ruled me. The theme was Finn and Tessa's idea. They've decorated the front room with white sheets and candles, giving it a ghostly air.

'Is your boyfriend coming?' Steve asks, as we clear the kitchen, laying out the borrowed glasses and paper plates for the veggie curry Finn concocted earlier.

'I'm meeting him at the station later.'

I'm not keen on Steve. If we'd had a vote about inviting him to move in, I would have voted against, but I abdicated responsibility to Vic and she still thinks he's OK. What happened after Paul dropped out was this: Vic put up spare room notices on various boards at uni, but there was hardly anyone around in the summer, so she ended up phoning the landlord, Mr Soar, to see if he had anybody looking for one room. Steve met Vic for a coffee and she thought he was OK, so Finn, Tess and I agreed to him by email, sight unseen. Steve's good looking in a square-jawed sort of way, but has a bad haircut, a cheap, shaggy look. He doesn't smoke or do drugs, but I try not to hold that against him.

Aidan rings up to say he's missed the train. I tell him there's another one in an hour. From the way he mumbles I suspect he's only just got out of bed. At seven in the evening. I don't really have a boyfriend. I have this guy I've met four times who emails me occasionally and is useless on the phone.

'We've got a fortune teller coming,' I tell him. 'You can't miss that.'

'OK.'

The fortune teller was another of Finn's ideas. Turns out Finn knows somebody who does Tarot and takes it all quite seriously. We're putting him in my room. I think Aidan would make a good fortune teller. He'd look great in a turban, like that famous photo of Rudolph Valentino. And I can't think of another career he's suited to, unless he has a hidden talent for acting.

When we've finished in the kitchen, Steve helps me sort out my room (Steve's room is being used for coats, so doesn't need much attention). I have bought mosquito nets, actually net curtains, from a stall in Victoria Market.

'I thought your boyfriend would be here by now,' Steve says. We are attaching the nets to the ceiling so that they float down, creating an intimate space at the side of the room.

'He's on his way.'

'Hold on. Finishing touch.'

Steve replaces my low energy light bulb with a red one, making the room feel like a brothel.

'If he gets here soon, you could have some fun in here before the fortune teller arrives,' he says.

'Or after they've gone,' I say.

'Why wait?' He slides his hand around my bottom and, squeezing it, pulls me towards him. Before I pull away, he kisses me.

'I'm going to pretend that didn't happen.'

'I'll bet you're good at pretending.' He clears off before I can hit him.

I have a quick shower, then put on my short black dress. We've urged guests to wear white, but white doesn't suit me.

There's an Indian rug over Finn and Tess's bed. A friend of Finn's has lent them a goldfish tank that lights up and they've placed it on the chest of drawers. When they turn off the main light, the tank appears to contain bright blue water and is backlit in such a way that the bubbles floating to the surface reflect a kaleidoscope of light from the exotic tropical fish. In the corner of a tank is a starfish. No, two. They cluster around an orange plant with delicate, coiled leaves. The fish seem oddly static. Ah, I see.

I knock, but Vic won't let me into her room. She's taken the TV, DVD player and everyone's laptops in there. Vic is a Fine Arts student, so I'm expecting some sort of installation. She was carrying round a video camera earlier in the week.

'Wait there a minute,' she calls, and I wait until a hand reaches out, holding two doves. 'For later. One for you, one for Aidan. Or you can have them both if he doesn't turn up.'

'You're a star. Thanks.'

The kitchen is full of party food — pizza, cheese, bread, potato salad — and cheap booze. I have a bottle of vodka stashed out in the open, disguised as white spirit, a trick I learnt from my mum. Last night, when I told the others we were bound to run out of booze by midnight, Finn said, 'Don't worry. Most of our friends aren't big drinkers.'

The party begins. The people who live in the house cluster in Finn and Tessa's room. A circle forms. New arrivals are introduced, though not by me. I want to feel sociable and toy with taking the e. I step back from the circle. Someone tells a joke. When Finn laughs, his whole body seems to shake, as though his back were made of rubber. Steve joins me.

'You're always on the edge of things, Allison. Why is that?'

I shrug.

'Taken your birthday present from Vic yet?'

'How did you know about that?'

'She offered me one. I don't need drugs, though I'd have been tempted if I thought she was trying to get into my jeans.'

'You never know,' I tell him, wanting to fuck with his head. 'You might have more luck with her than me.'

'But she's...'

'Nobody's sexuality's cut and dry. I'll bet you've done it with a bloke.'

He flushes. 'What gives you the idea...'

'You're easy to tease,' I tell him. 'Who did you invite tonight?'

'Nobody special. You think I'm a tart, don't you?'

'That's one word for it.'

'I'm making up for lost time,' Steve tells me. 'I used to be shy. Put women on a pedestal. Then I got here and found there were lots of girls who liked to get drunk and fuck. And I found I was very good at the fuck bit.'

'Modest too.'

'Take an e. You'll like yourself more on it.'

'That's a very cold thing to say. That I don't like myself.'

'No it's not. I can't stand people who think they're great. It's OK if other people think you're great. I think you're great, Allison.'

'I think you're drunk, Steve.'

'Only a little.'

The doorbell rings and I go to answer it. Aidan is not going to show up, so I neck the dove on my way, then open the door to find Mark and Helen. I had to invite them to the party but hoped they wouldn't come. Two worlds collide on my doorstep.

Helen is wearing white, as requested, and makes a bitchy comment about my black dress. She has lost weight since September and her hair is spikier. She looks less wholesome, but no less impressive. Mark kisses me on the cheek. He thinks Helen is going to dump him, he told me when we met for coffee. Things were fine when they were in West Kirby but here, they struggle to connect. They've been going out for fifteen months now. I told him he was being paranoid.

'Here. Late birthday present.'

I unwrap the oblong package he gives me. It's a jigsaw, a map of the world. Only Mark knows how much I like jigsaws.

'That's wonderful.' I give him a small hug. 'I'm going to put this safely away in my room. Booze is through there.'

'Is Aidan here?' Helen asks.

'No. I don't know if he's coming.'

'Right. Only I thought...'

I don't want to hear what she thinks of my seeing a mad

murderer, so give her a chilled smile and shoot up to my room.

After them, the deluge. People pour in. I hear the new arrivals as I'm coming up on the e. My head throbs in a nice way. I stop caring about Aidan's absence. I don't need a boyfriend. I'm sufficient unto myself. We all are.

I've taken e twice before, but before tonight, only a half. I was cautious. I still am. I convinced myself that I had a good time but, looking back, it could easily have been auto-suggestion. I felt like I thought I was going to feel. I'm not like Steve, anti-drugs, but I don't like being out of control. Speed doesn't seem to agree with me. Skunk is as far as I want to go. Ecstasy might be class A, but people treat it more like spliff. Only this feels a lot stronger than any spliff I've ever smoked. And I'm still coming up.

I put the jigsaw by the side of my bed then lie down beneath the mosquito net, waiting for my head to straighten itself out. Somebody comes in with Finn. He has a rich, plummy voice, like that guy from the "Carry On" films whose name I would normally remember.

'Let's put the books here,' the voice says.

'I'll take names,' Finn tells him. 'When do you want to start?'

'Give me fifteen minutes or so, dear.'

I hear some shuffling, then the voice addresses me. 'Oh, there's somebody in there.'

The nets part a little.

'Hi,' I say, 'I'm Allison. This is my room.'

'Stuart. Do you mind me arranging my things?'

'Go ahead,' I tell Stuart, who has a fat neck, partially concealed by a silk scarf, and a large, shaved (at least I presume it's shaved) head. 'I'll get out of your way before you're ready to begin.'

'Thanks.'

He doesn't close the curtain properly, so I watch as he switches on my desk lamp, then points it at the floor. A pile of books he's brought with him are arranged under the lamp's beam. The *I Ching*, *The Golden Bough*, *The Doors of Perception*. I hope nobody thinks that crap belongs to me.

'Something for people to read while they wait for their consultation,' Stuart tells me. 'I'm going to put some music on. Is that OK? The idea is that nobody overhears.'

'OK,' I say, feeling like a patient talking to a doctor who is about to perform a minor operation. Stuart presses 'play'. Birdsong. Ambient drones. Waves. A distant church organ. It's oddly peaceful. I hear Stuart returning downstairs.

I am higher than any plain. I walk on stars. Why should I be like you, earthbound? Look at the stars! Look at the moon! What holds you down?

This, this is infinity, and I am in it. I look down on the world and all I see is bluey green water, occasionally scarred by a continent. Then the picture is blurred by clouds, lots and lots of clouds.

Now I am moving further and further away, travelling at enormous speed. They said, they said that space was quiet but no, no it has a music all of its own and I would listen to it for all eternity, for I am

'Allison?'

'Aidan?'

I see a smiling face in a turban and, for a moment think that it's Aidan, but no, it's Stuart again, and the person speaking is Finn.

'Sorry, Allison, were you asleep? Stuart's ready to start the Tarot readings.'

'Tarot? I thought he had a crystal ball.'

'We've got a big waiting list already,' Stuart says. 'But since this is your room, I can start with you, if you want.'

'I'll pass, thanks.' As far as I'm concerned, Tarot readings are only one step above ouija boards.

'Probably a good thing,' Finn says. 'The natives are getting restless.'

He begins to organise. For a budding hippy, he's surprisingly bossy. One person joins Stuart under the nets. A second waits in line beneath the lamp, by the speakers, getting in the mood I suppose you'd call it. A third person, a girl I vaguely recognise, lands herself on the other side of my bed.

'Oh, cool,' she says. 'A jigsaw!'

'Nice one, Allison,' Finn tells me as I watch her open the box.

I stumble downstairs after Finn, who squeezes my arm.

'I'm sorry Aidan didn't make it,' he says.

I hate it when people are sorry for me.

'Hold on,' he says, when we reach the first floor, and opens the door to Steve's room. I'm trashed, or I wouldn't follow him inside. I hope he isn't going to kiss me. Steve was bad enough, but at least he doesn't have a girlfriend. Finn has Tessa, who I quite like, though I'm not sure how much she likes me. Finn pulls a wrap out of his pocket, then a credit card and a cut off piece of drinking straw.

'Have a bit of this,' he says.

'What is it?'

'Sulphate. Good stuff, I promise. Pharmaceutical grade.'

'I'm not sure,' I say, thinking of the last time I took sulphate, though that was supposed to be coke.

'It goes brilliantly with the e. Trust me, I'm a doctor. Nearly.'

'OK.' I snort a two centimetre snail trail of white powder

up my left nostril. It burns, but not in an unpleasant way. When I follow Finn out of Steve's room, we pass Mark on the stairs. He gives me a funny look. Acting oblivious, sniffing loudly, I tell him which door is the loo.

'I'm heading for the chill out room,' he says.

'I don't need to chill out,' I tell him. 'I feel like dancing.'

In the front room, I replace the techno with a full-on pop/rock mix CD Mark made two years ago and turn up the volume. This drives out the chatterers and smokers. For a couple of minutes, it's only me and Vic dancing, giggling and throwing our arms around, hugging each other. Then a Clash song comes on and half a dozen more people charge into the room. By the end of the number, it's heaving. Britney Spears follows, one of those great juxtapositions that Mark's so good at, and nobody leaves. We're throwing ourselves around even more. I'm dancing like I'm normally far too self-conscious to, sweating like we're in the Tropics, giving it up for every number, even the ones I'd normally disdain, until it's gone midnight and I'm thirsty as hell. I head into the kitchen to see if there's any beer left. There's plenty. Finn was right, most of this lot really aren't big drinkers.

I need to cool down, so I open the bottle of Grolsch then step outside, into the dark yard, closing the door behind me. I smell strong weed, which always makes me think of... I hear a small, familiar cough.

'Aidan?' I step forward. He's hiding round the corner.

'Happy birthday.' We hug.

'How long have you been here?'

'A while. I saw you dancing. You seemed to be having such a good time, I didn't want to interrupt.'

'You could have danced with me.'

'Not my thing. You know that.'

I suppose I do. 'Have you not brought a bag, a coat?'

'I left them in the room with the other coats. I wasn't sure which was your room.'

'Top floor. That's where the attic usually is, remember? But it's pretty weird up there at the moment.'

'Weird is good,' he says, and I begin to jump up and down with the excitement of him being here. Then I remember something.

'Here,' I tell Aidan. 'I've been saving this for you.'

I hand him the e. He swallows the pill without asking what it is.

Aidan is surprisingly sociable while he's coming up, answering Finn's polite questions, praising Tessa's kaftan.

'He's lovely,' Vic tells me. 'I like the shy ones too.'

Finn offers him some sulphate, but Aidan declines. 'My sleep patterns are strange enough as it is,' he explains politely. Then he stares at the fish tank, transfixed.

'One of them's dead,' he tells me, pointing to a goldfish that's floating on the top, next to a half smoked cigarette.

'Sorry to spoil the illusion,' I tell him, lifting out the plastic fish, which has come loose from the stick it's fastened to. At the other end of the stick is a sucker, attached to the bottom of the tank. I replace the fish and remove the butt.

'Show me your room,' Aidan says.

I take him up there. Beneath the mosquito net, Steve is getting a reading. A willowy girl with long, brown hair is doing the jigsaw.

'Mark and Helen gave me that,' I tell Aidan.

'Mark and Helen are here?' Aidan gives me a sideways, slightly alarmed glance. I remember what he said about why he wouldn't return to university. *Everybody knows*. I don't think Mark and Helen will say anything to anyone about him, but if I tell Aidan this it will sound like I think he ought to hide what happened. And I could be wrong. Also, I don't want Steve to overhear us discussing this. I get the sense that Steve is like me: sharp, even when he's off his face, even when he's meant to be talking to someone else.

'It's all cool,' I tell Aidan.

'Let's help with the jigsaw,' my boyfriend suggests. As we sit down, someone else arrives, a friend of Vic's called Tina. The four of us set to the jigsaw as a team, locked in negotiation, progressing quickly. Pieces are spread out on every available bit of carpet. We dredge our brains for fragments of geography. Where are Dakar, Fiji and Kilimanjaro in relation to other places? The girl with the long brown hair is called Persia. When she gets up for her reading, Steve takes her place. Then Tina says to her:

'Actually, I'm next. Finn's got a list downstairs.'

'But I've been waiting,' Persia starts to say, then realises how uncool it is to whinge. I describe Finn to her.

'Put me on the list too, would you,' my boyfriend says. 'Aidan.'

Persia goes off in search of Finn. I introduce Steve to Aidan. They shake hands like public schoolboys. Stuart gets out of my bed.

'Need to pee,' he announces and hurries out of the room. As soon as he's gone, Steve starts giggling.

'I can't believe anyone takes that stuff seriously,' he says. 'Where does he get off doing it? It's not like anybody's paying him.'

'I think he wants to get into TV,' Tina tells us from her spot on my mattress.

'It's not about Stuart,' Aidan says. 'It's about the cards that you're dealt.'

Sensing his seriousness, Steve starts to ask Aidan about comics. That's the one thing I've told Steve about Aidan, that he collects American comics.

'You must be into *Sandman*. Have you read *Death: the high cost of living?*'

Aidan has, but he has nothing to say about it. He passes Steve a spliff. My room will reek of smoke when we go to bed later. Persia returns and squeezes next to Aidan.

'You're after me,' she tells him. 'We've got the last two spots, after Tina.'

I open the skylight a crack so that some of the smoke escapes. Aidan and Persia set about the jigsaw. Steve's lost interest. So have I. Stuart returns and deals the cards.

'Ah,' I hear him say. 'Now this can mean...'

'I'm going down to the chill-out room,' Steve says.

'I'll come with you.'

'You'd better watch out,' Steve tells me halfway down the stairs. 'Persia's seriously into your boyfriend.'

'It's OK,' I tell him. 'I got there first. Aidan wouldn't encourage her.'

'Come in here a minute,' he says, as we pass his room. I follow him inside, thinking he's going to offer me some more speed, then remember that he doesn't use drugs, or so he says. He pushes the door to, then presses me against it, kisses me hard. Shocked, I let him. Only when I feel his hard-on rubbing against my groin do I push him away.

'Just because somebody got there first doesn't mean you have to stay with them,' he tells me. 'I'm really into you.'

In the silence that follows, we both become aware of movement beneath the coats.

'Hey!' Steve says. 'That's my bed you're using! Get a room, why don't you?'

While he's distracted, I leave.

Mark's in the chill-out room, sat next to Helen. Somebody's asleep on Vic's bed. Trance music is playing and there is a computer screen mounted in each corner of the room, on chairs or shelves. Steve comes in and moves a laptop so that he can sit down. Its screen is showing a glass of fizzy mineral water, lit from behind. Each bubble is a brilliant balloon. The screen opposite us shows an open fire, burning. I wonder where Vic found a real fire. Mark sees me looking at it.

'Kind of warms the room up, doesn't it?'

'Kind of.'

'Enjoying yourself?'

'Yeah. Especially now that Aidan's here.'

'Aidan's here?'

'Upstairs. Doing the jigsaw you gave me. It's a big hit.'

'It was meant to be just for you.'

I give him a smile. Helen lifts her head. 'We're heading off soon,' she says. 'Feeling a bit trashed.'

I look at my watch. Ten past two. The last couple of hours have flown by. On the video screen next to Steve, the glass of water is nearly flat. Then it vanishes. A moment later, another glass of effervescing water appears. Or maybe it's the same one, on a loop. I get up and hug Mark goodnight, thank Helen for coming, say I'm sorry we didn't get much time to talk. I mean it as I'm saying it. Helen says we must get together, just the two of us. What for? To discuss the magic that is Mark? She gives me her mobile number.

Downstairs, the dancing has fizzled out and the beer is all gone. I make myself a vodka and coke and pour another coke for Aidan. Upstairs, Aidan is under the mosquito net. Persia is still doing the jigsaw, aided by Vic and Tina. I can't hear what Stuart's saying to Aidan. They sound serious but fuck it, this is my bed. I even bought those net curtains. I reach into the confessional.

'I thought you might like a drink.'

'Bless you,' Stuart says. 'I'm gagging.' He takes the coke before I can explain that I meant Aidan. I step back out, look at the map of the world for a moment. They're nearly done. I can tell at a glance that there are two pieces missing, but the others haven't noticed yet. I'm not going to tell them. I'll need to start coming down soon. There's all this energy surging through me and I need to channel it, into dancing or, better, sex. Maybe a joint will help. I go back to the chill-out room.

'Where's Aidan?' Steve asks.

'Still having his reading.'

Steve gives me an inscrutable look. I want to challenge him, to ask what right he has to be so pleased with himself, but this is the chill-out room. Conversation, except of the most desultory kind, is frowned on. So is making out, although a couple of Vic's friends are clearly unaware of this. Or maybe it's me who's unaware. Three of the four screens are now showing porn — straight, woman on woman and man on man. They're kind of fascinating. I've never watched real porn before, apart from fragments on the internet. I'd better get away before Steve gets the wrong idea. On my way out I lean over and tell Steve something that he may find useful.

Going up the stairs, I pass Stuart coming down.

'That boyfriend of yours, he's seriously fucked up. You do know that?'

'You mean his cards are fucked up?'

Stuart rolls his eyes. 'The cards are just a bit of fun. If I were you, I'd whisk him away from that femme fatale who's been eyeing him all evening.'

'Don't worry. I'm working on that.'

Steve joins me on the stairs. We agree to operate a pincer movement. In my room, everyone is searching for the missing pieces. I point out that they are almost certainly under the almost completed jigsaw.

'But we'd have to wreck it to find out,' Tina says.

'Let me know if you find them,' I tell her. 'I hate to do an incomplete jigsaw.' I reach out my hand to Aidan, who gets to his feet. 'I'd like my room back in a few minutes,' I say, in what is meant to sound like a grown up voice. 'Aidan and I have got some catching up to do.'

Persia stands, a blurred look of resentment crossing her face. She feels like she's been with Aidan for a couple of hundred years and had already assumed a kind of owner-ship. That's when Steve makes his move.

'Persia, I wonder if you could help me.'

I lead Aidan downstairs for another drink, another spliff. He might come over all vague, but he always has a big stash of ready rolled spliffs on him. We go outside.

'It's a nice night,' he says. 'Look at the moon. Look at the stars. Do you miss the sound of the sea here?'

'We can't hear the sea from my house in West Kirby.'

'Oh. Right.'

He's gorgeous, I think, but so impractical, so fucked up. What did he and Stuart talk about tonight? Do I really want to take him on? Do I want to be taken on? He kisses me.

'Where are we going?' I ask him.

'Stuart says the cards aren't definitive. The future's in my hands.'

'I should hope so.'

He holds my hand and I fall in love with him again. That is, I feel something like love, though this is hardly surprising given all the stuff pounding around my brain. In a few minutes, my room will be free. I can take Aidan up there, lock the door and make love to him beneath the moon and stars. Aidan chooses this moment to give me my present, an emerald eternity ring. He puts it on my middle finger for me.

'It's lovely,' I say. 'You're lovely.'

'You're the best thing that ever happened to me,' he says.

When we go to collect Aidan's bag and coat from Steve's room, the door is locked. The coat is on the landing and the bag has already been taken upstairs to my room. From the landing, we can hear Steve doing with Persia what Steve does best. Aidan giggles, something I've not seen him do before. We undress in silence and sink beneath white, translucent nets.

LIMERANCE

Tessa leaves post-it notes on the fridge. *Soya milk for my use only — please respect my allergies. Does anyone but me unload the dishwasher? Gas bill due.* Finn frowns when he sees Vic, who is the worst offender in the housekeeping stakes. I make a point of picking up a J-cloth whenever I'm in the kitchen at the same time as Finn or Tessa. So far, I seem to have them fooled.

As a household, we haven't exactly bonded. Things have been in decline since the party. Next day, Finn and Tessa did most of the clearing up before the rest of us got out of bed. Being medics, they work long hours so they resent having to do more. In addition, they're a couple, and two years older than us, so it's hardly surprising they don't want to hang out with me, Steve and Vic all the time. Or at all. Our shared Sunday meals dribbled away by November. Now it's February and they never join us down the pub.

Steve, since he kissed me at the party, hasn't made any moves. Tonight, he tells us that he has a job.

'I'm working the phones at a ticket agency in town. It's a prime deal. Once you've been there a month, you get free tickets for shows as a bonus. And you get to reserve paid tickets before they go on sale. So if you ever want to see anything at the Arena, Rock City, Rescue Rooms, the Concert Hall even, I'm your man.'

The free tickets are a temptation, but I expect other girls will get first dibs. These days, I see more of Mark than I do of Steve. I usually have Vic in tow, so nobody can accuse us of having a thing. Mark moans about Helen, who has a separate life she doesn't invite him into. I moan about Aidan.

'It's like having a virtual boyfriend,' I tell him in the Peacock.

'Did I tell you about my virtual girlfriend?' Vic asks and starts telling me about how she had her first encounter with another woman when she was thirteen. She used to spend all her free time on this website called *Second Life*, which sounds like a multiplayer version of *The Sims*.

'I have no way of knowing if she was really a girl,' Vic admits. 'Or a teenager, like her avatar. But the way I see it, who cares? You never really know what other people are like. You can't get that close.'

'Isn't that what's supposed to happen when you fall in love?'

Vic gives me such a disgusted look that I feel embarrassed to my core for using the word 'love'. Then she gives me a lecture.

'What people call *falling in love* or *romantic love* is better defined as *limerance*. It's an obsessive state that some people fall into. If one person gets it, they're seen as a stalker or a psycho, but if two people feel it equally for each other, that's what we call 'mutual limerance' or 'falling in love'. For most people, it never lasts more than a few weeks or months. It's a drag when one lover loses it long before the other, but it's also inevitable. Some people get limerance far more strongly than others and some get it much more often —

young lesbians especially, which is why I know a lot about it. Other people never feel it at all. Maybe they're the lucky ones.'

I've never heard of 'limerance' before and suspect it's something she read up this week for her Psychology module. Later, I look the word up on Wikipedia. Turns out she's got it right, near enough.

We smoke a joint.

'What is love?' I ask, digesting this new idea. 'Is it what's left after you've gone through the limerance period?'

'Better minds than mine have given up on that one,' Vic says. 'Maybe there's no such thing as true love. It's a convenient fiction that allows people to stay together after the limerance period. An excuse for marriage, having kids and all that shit. An antidote to loneliness.'

I muse on this for a while, then look at my watch. Shit. 'I have to go to work.'

I head off to Moxy's on Lower Parliament Street, in the centre of the city. I've started doing three shifts a week, serving shots to pissed-up local yokels who don't give a shit about finding love or limerance, just so long as the evening ends in a fuck or a fight. Sounds gross, but I quite enjoy it. We're so busy that it keeps my mind off other stuff.

Easter vacation. This is where it gets serious. I have coursework to finish and exams to prepare for. Together they're worth 30% of my final degree. I decide not to go home until I've finished two essays and message Zoe to tell her. I saw a lot of Zoe over Christmas, though I've not been round to her house since the party where I met Aidan. I don't want to run into her dad. Sometimes she phones. We talk about Aidan and she keeps me in touch with what's happening in West Kirby. I've never told her what happened with Bob. We're not responsible for our parents' mistakes, so why bother her?

A-level results day feels like a lifetime ago, but it was only 20 months. Time is relative. I'm more than halfway through my degree and those five terms passed in a flash. Distance is relative. West Kirby is only three hours drive away, but feels like the other side of the world. Yet if I don't get a job before I graduate, I might have to move back there.

Everyone goes home for Easter weekend except me and Steve. I haven't seen Aidan since Christmas. Some days, he feels more like a patient than a boyfriend. We email less and less. Last time I phoned, I only spoke to his mum. She said he was coming out of himself, a little. I persuaded Zoe to go over and see him (her news is that she's training to be an estate agent). She said he was OK with her, so maybe it's just me he's lost interest in.

They're short-staffed on the holiday weekend, so I do more shifts at the bar. The money's good. If someone had told me a year ago that I'd become adept at dealing with drunks and enjoy flirting with strangers, I'd have laughed. But I'm cool with it. Steve's still up when I get back from Moxy's, no matter how late. We have a drink together, though some-times I'd rather go straight to bed with a book. He doesn't try it on, just makes it clear that if I find myself free, he'd like to be front of the queue to ask me out. Which is flattering. He has enough women on tap for him not to be desperate to have sex with me. There've been at least half a dozen since Persia. But I haven't had sex with Aidan since the night of the party. I've never had regular sex, full stop.

The ticket agency quickly promotes Steve. He's on 'difficult calls', or 'complaints', as they used to be known: tickets that haven't arrived or turned out not to be as good seats as they were supposed to be. He can mollify anyone. And he's already started getting freebies. Tonight, when I got in, he asked if I'll be back from West Kirby in time to see a show at Rock City. If anyone else asked, this would be a date, but we're house-mates, so it's not.

'I'd love to, thanks.'

'You're not going to change your mind and stick around at home to see *Peter Pan*, are you? Because, you know, it's the end of next week and..'

'I'll be back. I've got loads more work to do that I need the library for. And I'm behind the bar again a week on Saturday. Anyway...'

'Anyway what?'

If I tell Steve I'm thinking of packing in Aidan, he'll make a pass at me. Tonight, I'm weak. I might succumb. Which would be mad, because we live in the same house and I don't like him enough to go out with him. He's arrogant and slippery and greedy, not to mention silly and adolescent sometimes. Also, I'm not the sort of woman who cheats on her boyfriend. I'm not. But is Aidan really my boyfriend when I haven't had a word from him in more than two weeks? I'd like to discuss Aidan with Steve because, despite what I've just said, he is a sharp guy. But to discuss Aidan honestly, I'd have to talk about the accident, which would feel like a betrayal of Aidan, who made it clear how much he hates it when people know.

'Anyway what?' Steve repeats, coming to sit next to me on the sofa.

'I don't know. Aidan's such hard work.'

'I can see that.'

'No, you can't. You don't know the half of it.'

'Then tell me.'

And, to my surprise, I do. When I'm done, he puts his arms around me and I press my head against his chest, cry a little. There's nothing sexual in the embrace. It's comforting.

'What should I do?' I ask him.

'I think you're in over your head. He needs a therapist. You need somebody you can have a laugh with.'

'Aidan has a therapist. He never tells me what they talk about.'

'You don't have to feel guilty about dumping him, because he isn't really your boyfriend. He doesn't behave like a boyfriend. He doesn't want that responsibility. So you don't have that responsibility either.'

I wipe my eyes. 'Thanks. You've helped me to clear a lot of things in my head.'

I never thought I'd hear myself say that but what he told me was true, and it took Steve to say it. Last year I told Aidan's sister, Anna, that I wasn't responsible for her brother. Only I didn't mean it. It's one thing to articulate something, another to believe what you say.

Steve kisses me on the forehead and wishes me good-night. Classy. He's already argued me into being unfaithful to Aidan. I'm feeling vulnerable and it wouldn't have taken much to get me into bed. Is he playing me, or being a gentleman? Is there a difference?

In West Kirby, it's the dumping season. Helen has finished with Mark, just as they were on the verge of booking flights for a summer getaway. Mark's upset, but hardly devastated. Turns out he's been seeing a bit of this girl, Ro, who's in his hall of residence. By 'seeing' he means 'screwing', once or twice a week. He tells me this in the Ring O'Bells on Easter Saturday.

Then he has the nerve to make a pass at me. When I turn him down, he's persistent.

'We ought to get back together. We were great before. Now's the right time.'

'Too complicated,' I say.

'Because of Aidan?'

'I don't want to talk about Aidan.'

So we talk about Helen instead. She has started seeing a third year — a public school, banking family bloke. Mark reckons he'll dump her in the summer, when he graduates, but I wouldn't bet on it. Helen's a catch. Mark and I get very stoned together and watch the original version of *Solaris* until three in the morning, cuddled up on the sofa. He sleeps in the spare room.

In the morning, after Mum has gone to work, he asks me to go out with him again. I say 'no'. I've always liked Mark, a lot, but I've never obsessed over him, never felt that limerance thing Vic was on about. I was infatuated with Aidan for a while, but I'm not any more. Trouble is, I can feel myself going that way for Steve, which is crazy. If I were looking for a new boyfriend, I'd be much better off with Mark than I would be with Steve, but I couldn't stand it if he dumped me to go back to Helen. After a few drinks, it's obvious from his conversation: he's still hung up on her.

'I'm going to see Aidan,' I tell him. 'You can have a lift home if you want.'

'To Nottingham?'

'Do you think of Nottingham as home now?'

'Home is wherever you are, Aly.'

He's the only person I ever let call me Aly. I give him a wry *don't pull that line on me* smile, then take him to his parents' home. It's a warm day with a fresh sea breeze. For the first time since I got the car, I have the windows down. When I drop Mark off, he lingers by the car.

'Finish with him,' Mark says. 'I'll finish with Ro and we can start up properly. Go off somewhere over the summer.'

Before I know it, he'll be suggesting that we move in together.

'You can't go back,' I tell him. 'No matter how much you want to or how easy it looks. We wouldn't last, you know. We're much more use to each other as friends.'

'Men and women can't stay just friends,' he says.

Aidan's mum and step-dad are surprised to see me. I haven't phoned to say I'm coming, because Aidan will still be asleep.

'He's still out,' Linda says. 'Are you early?'

'Out? It's only noon.'

'He's gone to church with Anna,' she says, cheerfully. 'It's the second time.'

'Wow!' Aidan's parents are Church of England which, according to my Irish-Catholic mother, makes them practically atheists. But Aidan isn't a practising Christian. We've had the secular conversation, the one where you establish common ground, that God doesn't exist and a lot of the world's troubles are caused by the misguided primitives who insist on believing in him yet won't tolerate those who don't believe in their own, bigoted way.

'He's come out of himself a bit,' says Keith. 'I managed to get him a job.'

'What kind of job?'

'Trainee Financial Adviser.'

Again, all I can think of to say is 'wow'. At university, Aidan did Philosophy and Psychology. He told me he wanted to be a don, or a poet. Or both. Not an accountant.

'Here he is now,' Linda says. 'Aidan, look who's here!'

That's when I get the real shock. Aidan's had his hair cut. All the curls have gone. His deep eyes are too big for his face, and his jaw looks too long. I don't fancy him any more.

Instead of going to his room, we go for a walk through the dull, suburban streets.

'That Tarot reading at your party made me think,' he says. 'It was bullshit, but it made me ask the big questions. I need to make peace with God for my sins. I need to earn my way in the world.'

'You don't believe in God,' I say.

'That was just arrogance. I knew I'd sinned. How could I believe in sin but not believe in God? I doubted because I was avoiding responsibility.'

'I'm not sure I believe in sin,' I tell him. 'I can handle the concepts of crime and punishment, yes, but not sin, not guilt. You can know the difference between right and wrong without having religion.'

'I suppose,' Aidan says, but that's as far as he wants to take this philosophical discussion. We walk in silence. Whichever of us speaks first will be the one to end it, I figure. I've only ever had one serious boyfriend and I finished with him. I ought to experience what it's like to be finished with. But Aidan doesn't say anything. He's too passive. I figure it was Huw who persuaded him to play silly games in the car. Aidan didn't have the nerve to refuse. Or the sense.

'You and me?' I say, when we're in sight of the house. 'There isn't one, really, is there? I mean, we're good friends, but...'

'Yeah,' he says. 'You're right, Allison.'

And that's it. No warm wishes, no 'thank you, stay in touch'. I will never get another phone call from him. The only mutual friend we have is Zoe and neither of us sees much of her at the moment. If I want to know what happens to Aidan in the future, I will have to google him and hope there isn't another Aidan Kinsale in the world of financial services.

I drive home without saying goodbye to his family. I feel bad about that, because I'm closer to Aidan's mum than I am to him. Dad says life's all about cutting your losses. I'm not that ruthless. But I'm learning to be.

STARTING
TO HAPPEN

'Why didn't you get here earlier? I wanted to see the support.'

'Traffic was murder,' I tell Steve. 'We can go in my car if you want.'

'There's no parking near Rock City. We might as well walk.'

'Give me a minute to get changed.'

'You look great as you are,' say Steve. He's bossy, and I can't be bothered to argue. Am I really thinking of going out with this guy?

Walking up the hill, we discuss coursework, something we never do in the house, where it's not cool to remind ourselves that we're students. We both have stuff to finish for a week tomorrow, the first Friday of term. Steve can't decide whether to do a dissertation next year or two modules.

'How were things at home?' I ask.

'Same old same old. You?'

'Helen dumped Mark, that's the big news.'

'Doesn't surprise me,' Steve says.

'Why not?'

'She can do better. While they're at uni, people try to trade up. Who's she seeing instead?'

'Who said she's seeing anyone? A third year, as it happens. His family's in banking. Helen spent Easter with him.'

'There you go,' Steve says. 'And did Mark try and get you to go out with him again?'

'You're a mind reader.'

Steve gives one of those irritating, smug grins.

'So... have you dumped Aidan for him?'

'No! Aidan and I did agree to finish though.'

Steve suppresses a smirk. We're passing the Falcon on Canning Circus.

'Let's have a drink,' he says. 'It's murder getting served at Rock City.'

'Won't we be late?'

'Nah. Main act never comes on before nine-thirty.'

I take his word for it. I'm keen to see the band but he got the free tickets. I ask for a small glass of wine, rather than beer. I know how hard it is to get to the Ladies at Rock City.

'So... you finished with Aidan but turned Mark down. Why?'

'It'd be like — I dunno — doing A-levels again. You can't go back, can you?'

'I guess not.'

I've decided not to tell Steve that Mark already had somebody on the side. But Steve doesn't ask any more questions. Maybe he senses I haven't made my mind up yet.

I'd like to sleep with Steve. I've fantasised about it. But Steve's girlfriends never last more than a week, more often a night. We'd have to live in the same house afterwards. Soon we each have to decide whether to sign a new lease for next year. And I'm enjoying things the way they are.

'How was it, breaking up with Aidan?' he asks, in his sympathetic voice.

'He hardly seemed to notice.' I tell Steve about Aidan's new haircut, his financial planning job. 'It was like he'd shifted personality. Totally.'

'That happens to loads of people after university. Some of my brother's friends turned straighter than straight.'

'Yeah, but this was Aidan, half an ounce of weed a week Aidan.'

'From what you told me, he always went to extremes.'

'Should we be making a move? Don't you want to get a good spot?'

'I always get a good spot,' Steve boasts.

Once we're inside the venue, though, it's heaving. The stairway to the main floor is blocked by shoulder to shoulder punters. Even getting to the bar is difficult. We push our way along a narrow passageway between the people at the back. At least Steve manages to get served quickly.

'You sure that's all you want?' Steve hands me a half of cider. 'OK, follow me.'

One hand holds his plastic beer glass above his head. The other grips mine. Somehow, Steve pushes towards the throng that is the dance floor, though there's no space for dancing tonight.

'Excuse us. Coming through.'

People frown and moan. Some emphatically ignore us, turning their backs and widening their shoulders. But nobody can really object. There are no reserved places. We could be returning to a spot we had earlier. I half stumble on unseen stairs but Steve jerks me upright. It's when we come to a stop that the problems will start. We thread our way from the right side of the stage to the centre, moving back as we go. At one point, Steve stops, and a bearded bloke taps him on the shoulder.

'Keep moving,' he says. Steve's blocking the guy's girl-friend. We push through until we're two thirds of the way back, dead centre, maybe fifteen feet in front of the mixing desk. The couple we stand in front of are in conversation with the people behind.

'Told you I always get a good spot,' Steve says.

There are plenty of tall guys in front of us, but I can see a mike stand between heads. I hope it's the lead singer's. On cue, the band appears. They go into one of my favourite songs and the crowd shifts slightly. Suddenly, my view is great. I think I will go out with Steve.

But not yet. I enjoy the not so subtle way he rubs against me in the bouncy numbers, pulling me in front of him so that he protects me from the crowd and I have an even better view, but also feel the heat from his body, feel his groin grinding against my bum. For both of us, the real thrill is in the chase. It's the race that counts, not the finishing line. If we get together, it won't last, I remind myself. And we will still have to live in the same house.

When we get back, Vic is there. She wants to know all about the show. I let Steve tell her while I go up to have a shower. Then we share a joint while Steve has a shower.

'He doesn't normally do that after a gig,' Vic says. 'Does he think he's going to get lucky?'

'It was very hot in there.'

'That's not what I asked.'

'We went as mates, not... you know.'

'But did you finish with Aidan, like you said were going to?'

I tell her about Aidan, and about Mark, and by the time we're done, Steve has returned.

'I'm shattered,' I say. 'I'll leave you two to catch up.'

I half expect Steve to come upstairs after me, but he doesn't. I lie in bed reading for what feels like an age, knowing he's just below me and it's down to me to make the move, not him. It feels like power. It feels like growing up.

EXAM
SEASON

I used to knock myself out at exam times in West Kirby, but then I had an incentive: to get away. Now I'm here, I don't know what I want to do in eighteen months' time. I only know that it doesn't involve going back home.

Finn and Tessa are moving out next month, getting a flat together. So Steve, Vic and I have to decide about the lease. There are a glut of new-build student flats all over the city. The others reckon on getting something cheap, though this house is about as cheap as it gets.

Steve has a friend who'd like to move in, which would only leave us one short. I'm not sure. Once Finn and Tessa go, we won't be able to use Tessa's room as the living room (the big shared kitchen is fine, but you wouldn't want to spend whole evenings in there). A lot depends on what Vic does. If she stays, then I'll stay. If she decides to get a place on her own, I'll do the same.

As summer term starts, I work late at the library, catch the last bus back from the campus. Sometimes, Steve's on it. We talk about work. He's asked me to a couple more gigs and

I've turned them down. I'm working three nights a week at the bar and need the money too much to switch. But if he asks a third time, I'll say 'yes', whoever the band is. I don't want to give him the wrong signal. I am interested, but I'm also distracted.

Tonight, when I get home, Steve's about to go out, work a late shift at the ticket agency. He's making tea and does one for me. We sit in the kitchen with the house to ourselves, something that rarely happens in term time. I consider ribbing him about how his one night stands seem to have come to a halt. I rehearse my inquiry. Is he working hard for exams or just going through a bad patch? But he manages to throw me.

'It's my birthday next week.'

'Really? How are you going to celebrate? Do you want us to throw you a party?'

'Nah. Wrong time of year. Have dinner with me.'

'Where?' I say, which, I immediately realise, amounts to acceptance.

'Somewhere good. I'll book a table. Thursday. OK?'

'I can hardly say "no", can I? But it has to be my treat.'

'No. I choose the restaurant, I pay. If you have a good time, you can take me out and pay the next time. How about that?'

'It's a deal.'

As he leaves to go to work, he kisses me. Not on the forehead, but on the cheek, which is a move in the right direction.

I have to rearrange my shifts to make the date, but they're OK when I explain it's my boyfriend's birthday. I buy Steve a DVD I know he wants to see. And a card with a cool quotation from Frank Sinatra. Then I buy myself new under-wear.

'Do you want your present now, or tonight?' I ask at ten in the morning. I have a lecture to go to. He is making scrambled eggs.

'Depends what it is,' he says.

'Here.'

He laughs at the card and gives me a big hug after opening the DVD, a short but moist kiss on the lips.

'See you tonight,' he says. Vic comes for her lift. I'd offered to take her in the car because she has to return some video equipment she's been using for a project.

'What was all that about?' Vic asks in the car. 'You're not having a thing with Steve, are you?'

'I'm having dinner with him tonight. It's his birthday.'

'Oh God, you *are* having a thing with Steve.'

'I don't know what I'm doing,' I say, and it's the God's honest truth.

'Me neither,' Vic says, and starts to tell me about her love life. She's got a crush on this guy in one of her seminars.

'Guy? Has he got a thing for you?'

'It's sort of crept up on both of us.'

'And does he know you're gay?'

'He knows I have leanings both ways and he's cool with it.'

'You never told me you were bisexual,' I point out.

'Everyone's somewhere on the straight-gay continuum. If you grade it one to nine, I'm a six or seven.'

'What would that make Steve?'

'A one or two.'

I'm forced to agree.

'Not sure about you though,' Vic says. 'Where would you

place yourself?'

'Dunno. Four maybe.'

'I won't rule you out then. Four and six make ten, a good number.'

'What are we talking about here? Bisexuality or numerology?'

After we've gone our separate ways, I think about what it would be like to go to bed with Vic. It's not that I'm bi-curious, as such. But I've thought about what it would be like to be with another woman, specifically Helen Kent, though I think that may have a little to do with wanting to go places that Mark has been. Maybe I ought to try it sometime, but I don't want to spoil my friendship with Vic. Whereas I won't miss Steve's company should things go wrong between us. Vic isn't worked up by the possibility of my sleeping with Steve, so why should I be? Maybe tonight will be his lucky night.

I'm walking to my lecture, revising my plans about what to wear, when my phone rings. My dad, probably pissed off that I didn't find time to visit him over Easter, despite the car he bought me. For a moment, I consider rejecting the call, but Dad rings so rarely, I figure this might be important.

'Dad, I've got a lecture in two minutes. Sorry I...'

'This is about your mother,' he interrupts. 'She's in hospital.'

It's touch and go, Dad says. Driving home, I have to pull over because I can't concentrate. Crying, I ring Steve.

'Bummer,' is all he says.

'I'm going to the hospital now,' I tell him. 'I'm sorry about the meal.'

'S'OK.' He doesn't offer to come with me. Why should he? We're not going out.

I don't know if I can do this. Maybe if I take the train

instead. It's all I can do to drive up the road, pack a bag. Dad said he'd meet me at the hospital. He reminded me that he has a young family to get back to. As if I needed reminding that Mum only has me.

I don't know how long to pack for. I have exams round the corner and feel guilty for thinking about them. I put a couple of academic books in the bag anyway.

I get in the car and start to drive towards the motorway. I'm crying again and can't see properly. I pull over on a double yellow line. Cars hoot as they pass me. I'm blocking a lane. I can't drive to West Kirby like this, yet I must. I don't know anyone who can drive me. No, wait. I do.

✠

Mark is already outside when I get to the hall of residence, his bag packed. A tall girl watches us go and, although I am upset, I wonder if she is Ro, the one he's been seeing on the side. But I don't ask.

We hardly talk on the drive. The weather is foul, with heavy winds and mucky rain. Mark has to concentrate hard. I wish the car radio worked. Halfway there the phone rings. I tell my dad where we are.

'Mark's driving me. Remember...? No, he's not. OK, so I won't see you there. Is there any change?'

'How is she?' Marks asks when he rings off.

'She's recovered consciousness. It's too early to say how serious the stroke was. Dad's going home. Mum recognised him when she came round and his presence agitated her.'

'I'll bet.'

'Maybe mine will, too.'

'Don't be daft.'

Mark has known my mum for three years, since the first year of sixth form, but he only ever sees her on her best behaviour. I have plenty of good memories of Mum, but none are from the last five years. Dad's affair, the divorce, the aftermath: these things might have brought us together, but Mum's closest relationship recently has been with the bottle. I always thought she would come through it, that she would sober up and I would finish growing up and we would become whatever an adult mother and daughter should be. Now I don't even know if she will survive the night.

I'm not ready to say any of this to Mark. All I can think about is whether she will still be alive when I get there. I am the only child of an only child. Her latest boyfriend fizzled out before Christmas. I am all she has. At least I have somebody who was prepared to drop everything else and come with me. Does my mum have a friend who would do that for her?

Even in sleep, my mother's face sags on the left side. Not yet fifty, she looks like an old woman. It's a cruel caricature. The doctor tells me she might make an eighty percent recovery. It all depends on her, how much she wants it, how hard she works at the rehabilitation, how willing she is to fight. I don't tell him that all the fight went out of her five years ago. All I ask is:

'How long before she can go home?' He hesitates before replying. 'A long time. Months, at least. And, you have to prepare yourself, maybe never.'

I sit with her for an age that, when I look at my watch, turns out to have been half an hour. I am guilty. Guilty for not loving her enough. Guilty for not making her look after herself better. All the drink, no exercise, bad diet, they all contribute, no doctor needs to explain that to me. Her father died early, after two strokes in quick succession.

'I hate hospitals,' Mark says when I find him in the waiting room. 'The smell, that tired green colour everywhere, the noise.'

'What noise?'

'It's more the absence of noise. All the good sounds are missing, you know? Gossip, music, laughter. How is she?'

I tell him. 'Will you come home with me?'

I don't have to tell him that I don't want to be alone. He hugs me.

'We can stay at mine if you can't face home.'

'I have to go. There'll be things I need to sort out.'

Mum had the stroke at work, which is how come they were able to get her to the hospital quickly, which saved her life. The house is as she left it. Mail waits uncollected on the doorstep. Circulars. A postcard from someone called Jill. *Croatia is lovely.* A black cat scurries to the side of the fridge and starts whining. There are two empty bowls. I fill one with water, the other with horsemeat from the fridge. How long has Mum had a cat? Next to the cat food, there's a bottle of white wine, half full. I pour Mark and I a large glass. We're both hungry. He makes beans on toast while I phone Vic, who'd heard the news from Steve and left me a message. No messages from Steve. I think about ringing Dad but don't.

'Where do you want me to sleep?' Mark asks, later.

The spare bed isn't made up, and neither is the one in my room. I change the sheets on my mother's double bed. It's my bed for now. I ask Mark to sleep with me.

'Just sleep. Just hold me, please. I need to be held tonight.'

I'm not sure if I really mean this, but Mark takes me at my word. We cuddle for a minute or two, him in boxer shorts, me in T-shirt and knickers. He falls asleep with my left breast as his pillow. I don't. My mind races. After a while, he's heavy on me. I turn over, pulling myself from beneath him, then drag his free arm around me. He seems to understand what I want and snuggles up to me without waking. His warm, steady breathing on my neck soothes me, but I still can't sleep. After a long while, the door squeaks, and I curse myself for not closing it properly. I will have to get up, or it will bug me, but if I do, I will lose Mark's tender embrace.

There's another noise, a rapid, heavy padding, then the cat jumps onto the bed. Mark doesn't stir. The cat curls itself into a ball on top of the covers, beside my tummy. It begins to purr.

Protected on both sides, I cry for a while, then something inside me clicks and I am able to fall into numb, dreamless sleep.

In the morning, Mum is awake but doesn't recognise me. She seems more familiar with Mark, although it's hard to tell her smile from her grimace. I try to talk to her but we were never too good at casual conversations even when she was all there.

'This is hopeless,' I tell Mark outside the hospital. 'I don't know what I'm supposed to do.'

'You ought to talk to your dad. There's stuff to sort out.'

He's right. I need to talk to my dad or a solicitor and since my dad works with lawyers I'd be foolish not to call him. I haven't got the money to pay a solicitor or the time to queue for an appointment at the Citizens Advice Bureau. I phone Dad at the office and he agrees to come over in his lunch hour.

'What's he like, your dad?' Mark asks. 'You never talk about him.'

'Not a bit like you.'

I mean this as a compliment but Mark takes it weirdly so I elaborate.

'He's a couple of years younger than my mum. They had an affair when she was my dad's secretary at this firm of accountants in Hoylake. Dad was with his first wife, who he met at uni. Then Mum got pregnant with me and he did the decent thing. He got a divorce and married Mum as soon as he could, when I was six months old. Fourteen years later, he did the same thing all over again, although this time he waited to marry his secretary before he got her pregnant.'

'You told me some of that before. But what's he actually *like*?'

'He's my dad. I used to idolise him. Then I didn't. I don't know what he's like, not really. Stick around. You'll meet him.'

Dad shows up and proceeds to treat Mark like he's my boyfriend even though I said on the phone that he's not. We talk about money, about means tests, power of attorney, disability allowance, pensions. Dad offers to look through all of Mum's personal papers but I know how betrayed she'd feel if she found out that I'd let him.

'I'll do it. Just tell me what to look for.'

Dad talks about how to hide money, if the worst comes to the worst, about forging signatures and closing down accounts so the government can't take everything Mum has to pay for nursing home fees. It's too much information, too soon.

'There's nothing we can do about the house, I'm afraid. Your mother could linger for years, until all the money's gone. Do you know how much you're allowed to have before the means test kicks in? Fuck all.'

'Why are you writing her off so quickly?'

'Somebody has to look at the dark side. It's your interests I'm protecting.'

He takes a look at the Mini he bought me, silently remarking the two scratches I got while trying to park. Then he makes polite conversation with Mark about his course, his parents, when we are going back to Nottingham. After he's left, I ask Mark if Dad was what he was expecting.

'Not really. He reminds me of that bloke in your house, the one who's so sure of himself.'

'Finn?'

'No. The other one. Steve.'

'Steve's nothing like my dad.'

'Your dad seems all right. I mean, obviously he cheated on your mum and all that, but if you damn all the people who've cheated, it wouldn't leave many, would it?'

We're on shaky ground, for I know that Mark cheated on Helen with me, and with Ro, but I'm not going to let him defend my dad so easily.

'If people make a promise not to cheat, they should stick to it.'

'He was married to someone else when he got your mum pregnant with you. Would you rather he stayed with his first wife, persuaded your mum to have an abortion? You're holding on to a lot of bitterness, Allison. You've got to let it go. One day, he might be all the family you have.'

'Better to start from scratch, then.'

Mark gives me a funny look. When we started going out I told him I never wanted kids. I used fear of accidental pregnancy as one of my main arguments for not sleeping with him.

'Does that mean you want kids some day?'

'I don't know what I want.' I use the tears tactic and he gives me a hug. Then I ask him to take me home.

'To Nottingham or West Kirby?'

'Both.'

We get back to Nottingham just after ten. This was meant to be my first weekend going out with Steve, but he's nowhere to be seen. I invite Mark in for a drink (I pilfered a bottle of brandy from Mum's. She'll hardly miss it.).

'I'll take you again, if you want,' he offers.

'I can drive myself in future. It's just that, the other day, I was so upset.'

'We could go over in a week or two. I'm due a home visit before the summer break anyway. We could share the driving.'

'That'd be good.'

He finishes his drink. 'Do you want me to stop the night?'

I hesitate. There is no sexual nuance to his offer, but where Mark and I are concerned, sex is always an open question. If Mark stops the night, and Steve finds out, he will assume that Mark and I are lovers, and that will do for me and Steve. I would be better off with Mark than with Steve. But how would I feel if Mark dumped me for Ro, or the return of Helen? We are better off as we are. Every girl needs at least one good male friend, one she will never sleep with or — even better — has already slept with, so the sexual tension is out of the way.

There's a whining noise from the basket in the corner of my bedroom. I let the cat out. It has long, wild hair streaked red and black and bares its teeth before seeming to recognise me. Tentatively, I reach to stroke its neck.

'It's all right,' I tell Mark. 'I've got company.'

MEET ZE MONSTA

Two months after the stroke, there's little change in Mum. When I visit, she barely knows I'm there. I keep going. I talk to her, more than I have talked to her for years. Not that I have much to say. I tell her about the cat. Monsta had no flea collar or name tag until practical Tessa insisted on both. She got named by default, after a PJ Harvey song, since I don't know what Mum called her. She can't take in a word I say, so the name of the cat is irrelevant.

The first three visits took me a week to recover from. Now my depressive dips last anything between an hour and a couple of days. You can get used to anything, they say. I'm not so sure. My mum was an attractive woman, even when she'd been drinking. You expect to see a pretty face fade,

113

not vanish in an instant. You try to make sense of it to yourself. I keep seeing that cliché from TV shows and public safety ads, the one where a central character steps out into the road without looking and is immediately hit by a car or a van. But at least they get to die instantly. Whereas Mum...

It's good that Aidan and me are finished, because he'd be no use at the moment. There's only room for one patient in my life. What's happening to Mum is at the back of my mind all the time. It's hard to remember it's not on other people's minds and act accordingly. Finn and Tessa have each asked how things are. Once. After that, they acted as though they'd done their duty and it's selfish of me to keep acting depressed. Vic has been better, but she has a new girlfriend, called Liz. Her recent crush on the guy in her seminar group is forgotten. When I want to talk about Mum, Vic encourages (or at least allows) me to talk, but her fake concern frown says I'm spoiling the party. So I've stopped talking to her about it.

That leaves Steve. He's solicitous, without being pushy. I see less of him than I do of Vic, because his course is nearly full time and he works three nights a week. But when I do see him, he tries to cheer me up. We go out for drinks and movies — he always lets me choose. And he never tries it on. Which is odd, because his endless run of one night stands has either ground to a halt, or, if he has conquests, they happen elsewhere. It's like he's waiting, with infinite patience, for me to come round to being his girlfriend.

I keep Steve and Mark apart, as much as possible, but when they brush into each other — like when Mark turns up half an hour early to drive to West Kirby — they bristle the way Monsta does when another cat appears in our back yard. Mark behaves likes this even though (he's let slip) he's still sleeping with Rowena, from his corridor, and has managed to stay friendly with Helen. It's not like I'm the only game in town. I'm not even in play.

Love's not a game. Rubbish metaphor. The sort of thing blokes say. What's that song on 'Back To Black'? If love is a game, then it's a losing one. My brain has been on autopilot since Mum's stroke. Brilliant preparation for my second year exams. Fearing them, I work as hard as I can. Even on half brain power, revising is the best displacement activity going.

Women are meant to care more about feelings than fucking, but my libido returns before my emotions. Last week in West Kirby, I asked Mark to make love to me. He obliged. I was grateful afterwards, but felt... diminished, somehow. He should be the grateful one, isn't that how it's meant to work? I'm not being PC, am I? Blokes aren't PC. Neither am I. But I don't think I'll ask him again. It felt wrong, sharing him. You shouldn't have to share lovers. Or share yourself.

Monsta sleeps in my room, curled up on the edge of the duvet. Often, when I'm revising, she nestles up in the warm spot between my tummy and my groin, nuzzles me. I can see why some women prefer cats to men. They're more reliable, for a start. And their eyes make them look enigmatic, intelligent. Which is more than you can say for most men.

Vic is talking about getting a flat with her girlfriend. They've been together, what? Five minutes. OK, three weeks. A month at most.

'It's only limerance,' I tease her. 'It won't last.'

'Nothing lasts,' she tells me. 'Get it while it's hot.'

That leaves Steve and me, working out what to do next year. Tonight, when I bring this up, he avoids the subject, asks if I want to go a festival. I say 'no'.

'I don't think I could do it, three days in a field, no

showers, far more rubbish band than ones you want to see. It's probably OK if you take enough drugs, but neither of us are that into getting out of our heads.'

'You're right.' He hesitates. 'Any change with your mum?'

'No. Any sudden change will be for the worse, the doctors say.'

'Are you going back there this weekend?'

'Can't. Got one more exam to revise for. You working?'

'Only on Sunday evening. Want to do something Saturday night?'

'Yeah. Whatever. That'd be nice.'

'I'll see what's on.'

'It's a date,' I say, pointedly. For you can only be miserable for so long. After that, you have to get on with life or be dragged under. This weekend, I probably ought to sleep with Steve. And if it only lasts a night, or a week, so be it. Steve's fun, and I need fun right now. Mark comes with too much baggage. Everything about him reminds me of home. Which isn't to say that I won't end up marrying him one day. I often think that. Other times I think that I'll never marry anyone, certainly won't have children. I'm far too selfish. Best to know that about yourself early on.

At nights I cry myself to sleep, but the pillow doesn't get as wet as it used to. I've even started talking to my dad on the phone, every week or so. Strange to be brought together by the woman that both of us couldn't wait to get away from. I'll never stop blaming Dad — he should have waited until I was older before he left. But I don't think about that much any more. You can't spend your life focussing on blame. Mark says the people who are happiest are the ones who think about themselves the least, who are more interested in other people. Yeah, right. I'll go off to do VSO for a year. When I come back, I'll be so grateful that I don't live in some hot as hell, poverty-stricken shithole that I'll spend the rest of my days ecstatically happy I'm not poor or ill. Unless, of course, I get poor or ill.

Maybe volunteering would do me good, but I can't do VSO when Mum's the way she is. She could linger like this for decades. Is it wrong to worry about where that leaves me? I often feel like I've spent my whole life on hold, waiting for the next thing to come along, forgetting to live. So fuck it, yes, I will sleep with Steve.

THE MEN
IN MY LIFE

My father likes Steve. He sees a well groomed guy who doesn't wear ripped jeans, desert boots or trainers, and has outgrown the adolescent acne that still plagues both Mark and me.

'How long have you two been seeing each other?' he asks.

'Not that long,' I mumble.

'We've been living in the same house all year,' Steve explains, 'but it took me until June to persuade Allison to go out with me.'

'I was seeing someone else most of that time,' I remind him.

'He wasn't right for her,' Steve says.

I wonder what Aidan's up to. The conversation shifts to my mum, who is still hospitalised. She has dysarthria, dyspraxia and dysphonia, the full range of tricks that a brain attack plays on its victims. The doctors now say she's unlikely to go home again. Dad thinks she should sell the house, but what does it have to do with him? I'm against it.

'Maybe she could rent it out,' I say.

'Then you'd have nowhere to stay when you come home,' Steve says.

'There're always friends.'

'And me, of course,' Dad says.

I have stayed in his house a grand total of two nights since the divorce. Neither went well.

'Another pint?' Steve offers. Dad insists on buying. He'll be over the limit, but that isn't my problem. I left the car at home.

'He's not so bad, your dad,' Steve says when we're alone. 'From what you told me I was expecting someone... sleazier.'

'Maybe you don't notice how sleazy he is because you're a bit that way yourself,' I say, and regret the words as soon as they're out of my mouth. Steve's not good at taking criticism.

'I'm only sleazy in ways you like,' Steve says, running his fingers beneath my shirt, lightly tracing a path from my bra strap to my knickers.

'Not here,' I tell him, though it excites me.

Dad returns with the drinks. He asks about my exams. The results were so-so. Nowhere near a first, which was under-standable in the conditions, but respectable enough.

'I think you did very well. Have you thought about what you'll do when you graduate?'

'That's what? A year away? Get a job, I suppose. Start paying off my debts.'

He doesn't press me further.

'What about you, Steve?'

'The ticket agency I'm with would like me to stay on, say

they'd make it worth my while, but I'm not so sure. Some kind of marketing, probably.'

Dad's mobile rings. He tells Ingrid that he'll pick up whatever she's asking for on the way home, then gets up to go, leaving half his pint.

'It was great to meet you, Steve. You seem to be good for Allison. I've never seen her with such a healthy glow. You two are very welcome to come and stay with us next time you're over.'

'Thanks,' I say, half heartedly accepting his kiss on the cheek.

'Waste not, want not,' Steve says when he's gone, topping up his drink with the remainder of my dad's.

✠

That's right, Steve and I finally got together. That Saturday night, just before the exams, I caved in. There was no significant quantity of booze or drugs involved. Just lust. We've been all over each other ever since, more than two months now. I worried that Steve's previous girlfriends never lasted more than a week, but he says that he was waiting to meet the right girl. Or, more to the point, waiting for me to realise that he was the right guy.

I don't know if he is the right guy. All I know is that we have sex two, sometimes three times a day. It's a standing joke with the others in the house. Even my period doesn't bother Steve. My father thinks I've got over what happened to Mum because I've fallen in love. But I'm not 'in love' with Steve like I was with Aidan, like Vic is with Liz. I reckon romantic love, call it what you will, is over-rated. I'm happy because I'm getting laid.

'What's his wife like?' Steve asks as we walk back to Beacon Drive.

'Mid-thirties. Pretty. Comes from a well-off, Swedish family. Doesn't talk much, at least not to me, maybe because she stole my dad off my mum.'

'Women don't steal. Men take.'

'It takes two,' I point out. 'Otherwise, you would have got off with me far earlier.'

'Not the same,' Steve says. 'If Ingrid hadn't had your dad, somebody else would. There are blokes who are determined to stray. It's hard-wired in.'

Steve doesn't usually talk like this, but he gets drunk quickly and the three and a half pints have made him voluble.

'Are you trying to give me a warning?' I ask.

His smile is almost bashful. 'I've got a high sex drive. That's why I saw so many other women when you wouldn't go out with me.'

'You were seeing different women every week before you made any kind of move on me.'

'What did you expect?' Steve asks, swaying a little.

'I expected you to find a girl you liked enough to stay with her, but basically, they were all one night stands. Oh, except for the black one. What was her name?'

'Jessica. She stayed for a whole weekend.'

'She was nice. Why couldn't you go out with her.'

'Jessica was great. She taught me a couple of things. I would have gone out with her, but her boyfriend was coming back. She only went out with me because she was pissed off with him.'

'So when you say *I would have gone out with her* do you mean you didn't *go out* with any of the others?'

'Not for five minutes, no. You're the only person I've been out with this year. You're my first serious girlfriend, full stop.'

I ignore this compliment, if that's what it is. 'So what does sex count as, if not *going out*?'

'It's just sex. We're young. We can do what we want. Don't tell me you've never had a one night stand.'

'I have. It was meaningless, in every sense, compared to what we have.'

'Sure, but a lot more satisfying than a hand job.'

'All you need is a hole to come in.'

'Some girls are like that, too.'

'How many? You'd know.'

'You've heard the story. An average looking guy in a bar asks every single woman he sees to sleep with him. On average, one in ten say "yes".'

'Is that what you did?'

'I come from a small village. Everybody there has known me all my life. There's no casual sex to be had. Whereas in Nottingham, I'm anonymous. If a girl turns me down, I'll never have to talk to her again. Most times, even if she says no, she's flattered. At least I asked. There've been a couple who turned me down one night in Mooch but come on to me another night, said they changed their minds.'

'Are you serious? You've spent all year going up to strange women and asking them to have sex with you? No chat up lines, no cosying up while you dance in a club, just straight up *fancy a fuck*??'

'Pretty much, yes.'

'And ten per cent said *yes*?'

'Better than ten per cent. One in seven, maybe, one in eight. And bear in mind, I never asked mingers.'

This is true. I met enough of his one night women to

recognise that he has taste. And Steve is well above average himself.

'Would you go out with a girl who's slept with as many men as you have women?'

'Not if she was stupid enough to tell me.'

On the way back from the pub, we stop at Zoe's. Three drinks in, I'm reckless, don't care if we run into her dad, not with Steve here to protect me. But we don't. Steve's not met Zoe before and, the way he flirts and teases, it's obvious he fancies her. Zoe is impressed.

'I wouldn't have thought he was your type,' she says when Steve's in the loo. 'He's so different from Mark and Aidan.'

'He wore me down,' I tell her. 'What about you? Seeing anyone?'

She hesitates, then tells me in a rush. 'After you finished with him, Aidan started texting me. I'd just quit uni, most of my friends were away, so I went to see him. Aidan, he's kind of like a project. He's much better than he was, more like his old self.'

'I wouldn't know how to tell.'

'He's even holding down a job, getting up in the mornings.'

'And are the two of you... you know?'

'He's not very pushy that way. Did you..?'

'I can count the times on the fingers of one hand. Maybe you could slip some Viagra in with all the other meds he takes.'

'What are you two giggling about?' Steve asks as he returns.

'Nothing,' I tell him.

'Literally,' Zoe adds.

'Show me,' I say later, when we're home.

'Show you what?'

'What you do to pick up women. Pretend you've never met me before. Think of it as role-play.'

'You did drama at school. I didn't.'

'Go on, try to pick me up.'

He puts on a ham movie actor voice. 'I'm Steve. Would you like to come back to mine and fuck?'

'You'll have to do better than that.'

'I don't always say "fuck". Sometimes I say "I'd really like to take you home with me. How about it?"'

'Better. What lines worked best?'

'The ones I made up on the spur of the moment. I'd start asking where we'd met before.'

'Come on,' I say. 'Do it properly.'

He leans forward and gives me an admiring look.

'Are you in my seminar group?'

'I don't think so. What course are you on?'

'Economics.' He grins. 'I was wondering...'

'What?'

'Whether you'd let me come home with you tonight. Or, if you prefer, we could go back to mine. I'd really like to go to bed with you.'

'I'll bet you would,' I say, and figure this is the nearest I'll get to finding out how he operates. 'OK, then.'

'Not convincing,' he says.

'Pardon?'

'They always do a double take. Sometimes they ask their mate over, get me to repeat myself.'

'And do you?'

'Of course. Except I add that I'd happily service them both, if they want.'

'And do they want?'

'That'd be telling.'

'And how do they say "yes" when they do say "yes"?'

'Most look me up and down, the way a man would. You can see them thinking about it. Sometimes they snog me, like it's a trial rental. I've ended up doing it in a toilet a couple of times.'

'Some must say "no". Do you get your face slapped a lot?'

'Never. Usually, they say "this is a wind-up, isn't it?" or "so and so put you up to this, didn't she?" They want to turn it into a laugh and I let them.'

I take him into my bedroom, onto the single, unmade bed. Thinking of all the women he's been with, far more than I guessed, is turning me on. It's not just him I'm undressing, it's all of them too. I like his honesty, his bravery about sex. Get it while you're young. Get it while you can.

Later, when he's sleeping, I do my email. There's one from Mark, checking to see if I'm around. He's seeing Helen again. No surprise there. Her new bloke gave her the end of term elbow and, reading between the lines, Mark immediately did the same to Rowena. If Steve is like my dad, as Mark once said, then Mark is like me — a little uncertain about things, private, lonely a lot of the time, anxious not to hurt anyone. He'll cling to Helen and treat her well, but she'll dump him again. This is one of the things nobody tells you about going out with people at university. You're allowed to experiment with sex the same as you are with drugs — different class, colour, sex, age, intellectual agility. But when you come out at the other end, the old rules still apply. People pair off with someone of their own social class. If you're exceptionally bright or beautiful, like Helen, you're allowed to trade up as high as you can get away with. Helen's parents belong to the golf club. Mark lives on a former council estate. He works as a caddy at the golf club. Enough said.

I suspect that Steve and I are even. I don't know what his parents are like. He never talks about them, or says much about the village he's from. I wonder when he'll take me home. If he does, I'll know he's serious about me. He'd say that renewing the lease on the house we share shows he's serious. We're moving into the rooms that Finn and Tessa share. Our turn to be the couple of the house.

I reply to Mark, agreeing to meet, saying I'll bring Steve with me, and it'll be nice to see Helen again. I don't want to see Mark alone, for he is my reserve guy, the one I will turn to when Steve bails out. And I am Mark's back-up girl. Neither of us needs to articulate this. All over the world, there are reserves waiting for their call up to the first team, the Love Eleven. Only nobody calls it "love". They don't know what to call it. I like Mark more than I like Steve but Steve excites me, and I like him about as much as I like myself. If he were a stranger and came up to me in a bar offering no strings sex, I might say "yes". We're not strangers, so I've no way of knowing. But we've both got strings now. Sooner or later, one of us is going to start pulling them.

THE OLD GANG

It was Zoe's idea.

'I can't go on holiday with Aidan on his own. You know what he's like.'

'You're the one going out with him.'

'I've already persuaded Mark and Helen to come.'

'Jesus, Zoe. I'd be going on holiday with my two ex-boyfriends.'

'But you finished with both of them. And Mark was so long ago. Steve doesn't look like the jealous type to me.'

'I'll discuss it with him,' I said. 'See what he thinks.'

'Persuade him,' Zoe said. 'It'll be like the old gang.'

'And I'll be the odd one out,' Steve says, when I put it to him.

'We were never really a gang. Zoe and Mark were at primary school together, but I've only known Aidan a year. And Helen, well...'

'I don't know.'

'We wouldn't have to spend all our time with them.'

I'm nervous about going on holiday with Steve on his own. Out of bed, we don't have that much in common. Anyway, he hasn't suggested that we go on holiday together. And I need to. I've had a crap year and I need to get away. Home is my mum. Nottingham is finals. I need to be elsewhere.

'It's not for long. A week, ten days at most. That's all any of us can afford.'

Steve's tight-fisted. It's taken me a while to work this out, but the signs are clear. The meals in restaurants haven't happened. He doesn't drive, and never offers to pay for petrol. He lives in the cheapest house going, has a decent part time job and is usually the last to buy a round. I have to make this holiday worth his while.

After three days, he agrees to go. What impresses me most is that he doesn't once display any anxiety about us being in close proximity to my two ex-boyfriends. They're no threat to him. That's how sure of himself he is.

How sure am I? On the plane, I can't help but make comparisons. Steve, while the shortest of the three guys, only four inches taller than me, is the most conventionally good looking. Aidan, even with his curly hair cut short, looks coolest. Enigmatic. Unlike Mark, whose open face is more footballer than rock star, and whose haircut is dated: mid-90's Britpop. Helen should tell him this, but to her he has become a comfort figure, a favourite family pet.

We girls compete too. Helen is way ahead in the tits and legs department, though Zoe, with her funky feather cut and artificial tan, competes in the glam stakes. She's already been mistaken for a travel rep, a career she has considered. I'm the odd one out here, prone to dressing down, with breasts you'd only notice if I went topless, which I have no intention of doing. Steve says I'm his ideal body type, that I look like a model (I'm not tall enough to be one), but I've already seen him ogling Helen's low top, hoping to chance on a nipple slip. On holiday, he might revert to type. I'll have to watch him.

Mark's brought some weed with him. It's double wrapped and concealed in a trouser pocket somewhere in his suitcase. No e's. He says they're easy to get on the island. And no need to be nervous. The 'nothing to declare' line at Customs isn't staffed. Within half an hour of our reaching the hotel, Mark's skinning up and passing the spliff along the balcony to me and then to Aidan, on my left.

'Should you be doing that?' I hear Zoe say.

A few minutes later, on my right, I can hear Mark and Helen making love. So can Steve. He feels me up. I'm not comfortable, having sex in such close proximity to the others, and, for once, I don't finish. Steve hardly notices. Mark is going to get some whiz so that we can hit the ground running. I hear him go out and come back. It takes him all of ten minutes. Everyone has some. Even Steve has a dab, but it doesn't suit him. He's even more confident than usual, annoyingly hyper. I thought speed might make Aidan more loquacious, but it has no visible effect.

From night one, a pattern establishes itself. We eat badly, neck a few beers and a couple of pills, then hit the clubs around midnight. Before dawn, we chill out on the beach or the balcony. Then we sleep until at least noon. Wander around, get a tan and/or screw in the afternoon, followed by a little more sleep, then the whole things starts up again. On the third day, I try to persuade Steve to rent a bike and explore the island, but he's not keen. Helen agrees to come with me instead.

'I wonder how Mark and Steve will get on without us,' Helen says as we leave the bike hire place.

'Me too.'

Then she swears. Her period has started and she needs to go back to her room.

'I'm sorry. It's early. This always happens when I go on holiday. I guess I'll have to cry off.'

I don't want to cycle alone, so I head to the beach to see if I can find one of the others. Aidan is on his own. I ask where Zoe is and he gives me a 'don't know, don't care' look.

'Helen's got her period and she won't cycle. Do you want to come with me instead?'

'All right,' he says. 'Give me five minutes.'

He drapes his towel around shiny shoulders and leads the way. I look at his wiry frame, his flat bum, and wonder how I ever fancied him. His eyes are duller these days, perhaps because the drugs he's on are working.

When we get to the road I start to worry. Aidan wobbles a lot and takes a while to find his pace. I haven't used my bike much since Dad bought me the car, but it's not a skill that deserts you. That said, Aidan, with his driving ban, isn't used to roads. I cycle cautiously, keeping a constant eye on him. He doesn't seem worried, or aware of my concern, but we can't have done more than a couple of miles when he suggests that we stop for a beer.

'I think it was somewhere round here that Nico died,' he says. 'She had a heart attack while she was riding her bike and fell off, hit her head on a rock. It was the rock, not the heart attack or heroin, that killed her.'

This is the longest speech he's uttered all holiday. I get him to explain who Nico was. He gets quite enthusiastic when he talks about the Velvet Underground, although not the way Mark does when he's talking about music. Maybe Zoe's right and Aidan is becoming his old self again. Only I never knew his old self and everybody keeps changing, all the time. Other people rarely notice this, because they're so wrapped up in themselves.

'You and Zoe seem good together,' I tell him.

'Zoe and Aidan,' he says, slurping Becks. 'We sound like a children's picture book. Zoe's great. I thought you and Steve would get together. That party at yours, I could see how much he wanted you. Even the next morning, when he was with that Persia girl, it was you he looked at.'

'She was more interested in you than him. I got Steve to take her off your hands. Maybe we should have swapped that night.'

'I wouldn't have done that to you.'

This is the most open conversation I've ever had with Aidan. He isn't like this with the others (except, I hope, Zoe, when they're alone).

'What about you, Aidan. What do you really want?'

He lights a cigarette and his eyes seem to focus on the middle distance.

'Not this,' is all he finally says, stubbing out his cigarette, half smoked.

Without discussion we get back on our bikes and head back to the beach, reconnoitring clubs and bars as we cycle past them. We've done the best ones in walking distance, but spot a couple which look smart enough to justify forking out for a taxi. By the time I'm back in my room, I feel like I've made progress with Aidan. We're mates, insofar as Aidan has mates.

From my room, I can hear Zoe giving Aidan a hard time for going off without telling her.

'You could have been anywhere! I was worried sick. No, I didn't think *that*. I trust you both. I thought Allison was with Steve, I thought... I don't know what I thought.'

Aidan's voice in reply is calm, soothing. I can barely make out the sound, never mind the words. Of Steve, there is no sign. Maybe he's out on the pull, checking his average 'yes' rate. The place is full of single women, so he should do well. I doze off. When I wake, he's in bed with me, his instant hard-on a sign that he's not been straying. I decide to relax and trust him.

✠

Afterwards, we shower together and he produces fresh drugs. For an abstainer, he's discovered a strong affection for e's and whiz. By midnight, we're flying. Even Aidan, never much of a dancer, is making shapes. Zoe, who usually restricts herself to a few puffs of spliff or half an e, is speeding like crazy.

'This is the best I've ever felt,' she tells anyone who'll listen. 'The very, very best.'

It's four in the morning and we're all on the beach with big bottles of San Miguel and Metaxa, smoking spliffs the shape of magic markers. The boys are talking bullshit at the speed of sound. We girls are more chilled out, but my head's still throbbing from the speed and e. The weed smoothes the edges but it'll be hours before I'm ready for bed.

It's Helen who suggests playing *Truth Or Dare*. Any other time, I would have put a stop to it, but I'm too fucked up to flash a warning sign.

'That's such a cliché,' Steve says.

'What is it you're interested in?' Zoe asks Helen. 'The truth or the dare?'

'I like to hear the truth,' Helen says. 'We're all friends, so the truth can't hurt us. It can only make us stronger.'

'Telling the truth gets people into trouble,' Steve says. 'It's dangerous. Sometimes, lies are all that keep people from beating each other up.'

'Nobody's going to beat anybody up,' Aidan says.

Mark is quiet. So am I.

'Is Steve always this middle-aged?' Helen, *sotto voce*.

'Who wants to start?' Zoe asks, before I can answer.

'Truth, no dare,' Helen says. 'Can I start?' She turns to me. 'Allison, do you still have feelings for Mark?'

Easy one. The speed makes me open, articulate. 'Of course I have feelings for him,' I say. 'He was my first serious boyfriend. I hope we'll always be friends. But I'm not out to take him off you. I'm with Steve.'

Helen opens her mouth to ask a follow-up but Mark stops her.

'Asked and answered. My turn. Steve, you're always dropping hints when the women aren't around. Now I want to know the honest truth. How many women have you slept with?'

Steve gives one of his lazy, arrogant smiles. 'You don't think I keep count, do you?'

'I'm sure you do.'

'We all do,' I add, and Steve grins. Then I tense up a little. He may be a slut but he's my slut.

'Why doesn't everyone have a guess?' Steve says. 'Make the game more interesting.'

'Good idea.' Helen gets out some green rizlas. 'Everyone

put their name and number on. Steve, you write it down too, so you can't cheat. Remember, total honesty. No exaggeration.'

'What about under-exaggeration?' Steve says. 'We're talking about full sex, right?'

Everyone writes a number. Strangely, I want to win. I calculate what Steve's told me about his first year in hall, average a conquest a week for term time, knocking off a few weeks for exams and illness. We hand the rizlas to Steve, who opens them.

'OK, here we go,' he says. 'In reverse order. Helen: one. Very funny. Aidan, twelve. Not even close, buddy. Mark. Twenty-five. Getting warmer. Zoe, eighty-eight. Who do you think I am, Hugh Hefner? But the winner, the one who gets the prize of my body tonight and the most significant digit on this illustrious list, is Allison.'

'What did you guess, Allison?' Helen.

'Forty-seven.'

'Show us, Steve,' Mark says.

'Come on,' Helen says. 'We all want to know what number Allison is.'

Steve hands over the rizla. Forty-three. Suddenly, I feel humiliated. Forty-two women before me. How many will there be after?

'My turn,' Zoe says. 'Mark, do you still have a thing for Allison?'

'Jeez,' Helen says. 'Are you trying to split us up?'

'Actually, I am,' Zoe says. 'In the long run, I think Mark and Allison ought to be together. He calms her down. She keeps him more... together. Nothing personal, Helen, but you know that Mark's only a stop-gap for you.'

'Notice she doesn't apologise to me,' Steve says, as

Helen strokes Mark's hair, murmurs something to him.

'Does speed do this to everyone?' Helen asks, 'puts them on a total honesty jag? I'm beginning to wish I'd never started this game.'

'Uh, Zoe and I took a little acid too,' Aidan says.

'And you didn't offer us any?' Mark says.

'I'm not sure I'd take acid,' I say. 'Too scary.'

'Too right,' Steve says.

'Obviously it wasn't acid,' Helen says. 'It was that truth drug they used in the fifties, sodium somethingtol. Go on, Mark, give your answer.'

Mark doesn't look at Helen, or at me.

'Realistically, none of us are going to be with the same person for the rest of our lives. I know Helen won't stay with me. And yeah, if I had to choose one person I already know who I'd like to end up with, it would be Allison. She knows that, at least I hope she does. But, you know, we'll all probably get married, have kids etc with people we haven't even met yet.'

'Wow,' Zoe says. 'Allison, what do you make of that?'

'I've already answered my question,' I say.

We all see at once that Helen is crying.

'Why?' she says. 'Why do people have relationships they know aren't going to last? I don't mean Steve and his one night stands. I don't even mean you, Mark...'

'Tired and emotional,' Steve mumbles to me, as Mark gives Helen a cuddle.

'Sorry,' Zoe says. 'I didn't mean my question to...'

'It's OK,' Helen says. 'It's just that, I thought he was going to marry me. I thought he was the one.'

Aidan clicks that she isn't talking about Mark and turns to Steve. 'I think it's your turn. Uh, me or Zoe.'

'This doesn't have to be about relationships, does it?' Steve asks.

'Please,' Aidan says, 'anything else.'

'Anything? The sodium pentothal reply?'

'Anything.'

'OK,' Steve says softly. 'Tell us what really happened, the night of the crash. Goes no further, just the six of us.'

'That's not on,' Zoe says, sharply.

'You don't have to,' Helen tells him.

I stare daggers at Steve, but he's not looking. He's staring at Aidan, who's staring back at him. Mark was rolling a joint, but he's stopped.

'All right,' Aidan says. 'I agreed to play, so I will. You got any of that speed left, Mark?'

'Isn't it a bit late?' Zoe says, as Mark gets the wrap out.

'I won't sleep tonight anyway.'

It's nearly dawn. Aidan takes a large dab, washes it down with beer, and swigs from the brandy bottle as he talks. It takes him a while to warm up, but when he gets going, his voice is clear, strong, even defiant.

'The thing was Huw's idea in the first place. I passed my test two months before him and we'd go driving. Just driving. No destination. Once we drove through the Mersey Tunnel stoned and I got disoriented, nearly crashed. After that, Huw passed his test and got given his own car, so he did most of the driving. He came up with the game one night when we were both off our faces. How close could you go without hitting? How fast? He hated slow drivers, that was what really got to him. If you were behind the wheel on a road with no speed cameras, you ought to go at a fair lick, not twenty-eight fucking miles an hour. So he'd get right up their backside until they speeded up or pulled over.'

'And if they didn't?' I hear myself ask.

'They always did. Or turned off. Or something. We didn't give them room to brake. Huw was better at it than me. I was worried about scratching my mum's car. Huw had a banger, he didn't give a shit.'

'What sort of cars did you tail-gate?' Steve asks.

'Anything, as long as we could see the driver. Young. Old. Couples. As long as there were no kids in the back. That would have been too creepy.'

'And didn't you get any retaliation?' Mark.

'How many questions is that?'

'You haven't got to the crash yet,' Steve points out. Aidan ignores him.

'There was one time, a car braked slowly and we hit the bumper. He pulled over, tried to block the road. Big, angry guy got out. But he'd left us room to get past him. We scratched his car as we went round. He banged on our boot but there was nothing he could do to stop us.'

'And he didn't report you to the police?' Helen.

'Huw always put mud on the plates.' Aidan pauses, takes another hit of brandy. 'The police made a big thing of that at the trial, that we always put mud on the plates. Said it showed premeditation. Like we were looking to kill someone.

'The night of the crash was just like any other night. We were at a loose end. I didn't have any weed. Huw wanted to go to a party but I wasn't up for it. I suggested the drive. I thought it might get my adrenaline going, make me more sociable.

'I think Huw suggested that I drive. Not a dare. More that he was growing out of it. He had a car all the time, while I hardly got to use my mum's. Driving was more of a thrill for

137

me. Technically, I wasn't insured to drive his car. That came up in court too.

'Sometimes, before, it was a random thing. We wouldn't do it or we'd start to, then drop back, turn off. That night, we were really up for it, almost like we'd decided it was going to be the last time, so it better be good.

'They had a big car, a Volvo. Neither of us could tell how old they were. I suppose that made their reactions slower. They were on the long road out from the golf club. Blind corners, lots of dips. They were doing 25, 27 tops. Huw got really pissed off when they wouldn't speed up at all. Then I started nudging them. Just tapping the bumper. And it had the required effect. They speeded up. We stayed right on their tail. Got up to forty, forty-five. Huw urged me to nudge them again, but it's harder to do a nudge once you get to forty. They were up to fifty when, suddenly, they start to brake and I ran into the back of them. Not hard, there was barely a scratch on Huw's car afterwards, but his brakes weren't as efficient as theirs and they had to keep going.

'If there hadn't been anything on the main road when they came out, it would have been OK. But there was. I swerved around the accident. You could tell it was bad. The woman whose car they hit, the airbag in her Polo came up and she was all right. Well, she started bleeding from the nose when Huw went to talk to her. She was in shock. Later it turned out she'd broken her forearm. She couldn't drive again for months afterwards. But basically, she was all right because the old couple only sideswiped her. After they did that, they went off the road, straight into the lamppost.

'Their car was twelve years old. It didn't have airbags, but that probably wouldn't have saved them anyway. They were going too fast.'

Steve breaks the silence that follows. 'How did they catch you?'

'I phoned the ambulance on my mobile. For five minutes, we were responsible citizens, looking after the woman from the Polo, putting out the red triangle from Huw's car. Then the police came and she must have said something because they arrested us both. She'd seen the way the old couple's car came out onto the main road, knew there was something odd going on. There were a couple of other witnesses. One of them talked about how terrified the old guy looked. He'd had heart surgery, his daughter told the court, thought he wouldn't live to see his second grandchild. And he didn't, because of us.'

'I got off lightly, mainly because I'd been sectioned by then. Huw's parents told him what he had to do to get off and he got off. He wanted to confess, he didn't want to dump me in it. Not that I gave a shit. Now I'm here and he isn't. Some dare, eh?'

'You can't beat yourself up forever,' Zoe says.

'Watch me try,' Aidan says. Then he quickly adds, 'Anyway, it's Allison's turn now. Who hasn't had a question? Zoe?'

Zoe and I look at each other. She's pale. I look at Steve looking at Aidan. They can distance themselves, these men, see their own lives in abstract. Maybe it's the drugs they're on, or maybe it's in their characters. Tonight, I don't like Steve much and I don't want to stay around Aidan. Why did Steve have to ask that question? We could talk this through but he's off his face and won't remember in the morning, though I will. I suspect Zoe feels pretty much the same.

'I'm ready for bed,' I say. 'Zoe, do you want to sleep in our room tonight, leave the guys to it?'

She nods and gets up. We leave without making eye contact, without saying goodnight. On the way back to my room, neither of us utters a word.

EATING OUT

Vic says she's moving out.

'It's not your fault, it's just the way things go. We were best mates, but now you and Steve are all over each other and we hardly talk.'

'You're exaggerating.'

'You didn't call me once when I went home in the summer, Allison. You didn't ask if I wanted to go to Ibiza with you.'

'That's because it was all couples.'

'Straight couples.'

'But you'd split up with Liz at the time.' They split up the week before they were meant to move into a shared flat, but they've since got back together. 'You'd have felt...'

'Exactly,' she interrupts.

'It's not like that,' I tell her, though I can see that it is. 'The first few weeks of going out with someone, of course you haven't got time for anyone else. That's inevitable. But we can solve this, make space for each other.'

'Too late, babe. I've already paid the deposit on the room. Mr Soar says he's got someone else waiting to move in.'

'Oh.'

'I never thought, you know, you and Steve,' she says, her voice oozing disappointment. 'I hope it works out for you.'

She's breaking up with me. I haven't had a friend formally break up with me since primary school. Friendship is like romance. It needs to be nurtured. And I haven't done much nurturing since Mum had her stroke. Vic didn't know how to deal with that. She turned to Liz and I turned to Mark. At least that's how I saw it at the time. Then there was Steve, waiting to become my lover. And, somewhere along the way, Zoe became my new best girl friend, only Vic doesn't know this, because she's never met Zoe.

Update: Aidan and Zoe are still together. Zoe thinks that telling everyone about the crash marked a major turning point for Aidan and, having done his worst, as it were, Aidan's seen that nobody got really freaked out, so now he can get on with his life. After that night, Steve said, "I can't believe you used to be into that guy." Otherwise, we never discussed it. Mark and Helen, meanwhile, are still in a sort-of-going-out state, but they're not living together. Mark has moved into the city. I said there might be a room in our house, but he prefers to live alone. Or, at least, not with me and Steve.

I hardly know the three new people who've moved into the house. Sometimes it feels like I'm living alone. Steve is out a lot. His course, unlike mine, is pretty much nine to five. He works three nights a week and Saturdays at the ticket agency. There are nights when my being behind the bar clashes with his nights off, so we don't spend that much time together.

Instead of making love twice a day, we're lucky to do it twice a week. I call it 'making love' but he never tells me he loves me. I never use the word either. Some people don't. That's cool.

The third time I complain that I'm not seeing enough of him, Steve's announces that he's taking me for a meal. He's booked a table at the Loch Fyne Oyster Bar, which is a posh seafood restaurant on King St. As we go in, I worry about his motives. It's a classic male move, or so Zoe tells me. Take the woman somewhere smart when you want to dump her. She won't dare kick off and make her humiliation public.

We get a table on the side, facing in. Steve asks for a special menu and I realise that he's got some bargain deal, with a free glass of house white thrown in. That's more like Steve. I begin to relax. The food is good. We order more glasses of wine. Steve is on good form, telling anecdotes about customers at the ticket agency, mentioning gigs we might go to, listening attentively when I explain a problem I'm having with an essay. I talk about Barthes and the death of the author and the lover's discourse, make links with how Vic and I used to talk about limerance.

'Remind me what limerance means again,' Steve says. So I do and he goes off on one about how romantic love is a concept invented by women. Steve has this irritating habit whereby he'll take in a new bit of information, or some theory that he agrees with, then act like he knew it all along — because, with his huge ego he thinks he has, he just hasn't put it in into words before. He then goes on to form an instant opinion about the topic. I've seen other boys behave this way in seminars. They think they know everything. At least, in a seminar, there's a lecturer to shoot them down, or expose their contradictions. Over dinner, I choose my words care-fully.

'You could be right,' I say, and hate myself for it.

We're finishing off our main course when I see him wince slightly, then aim a smile behind me. I don't turn round.

'Someone you know?'

'One of my tutors.'

A few minutes later, when I'm going to the loo, I notice a woman checking me out. She's a Helen type, athletic looking, with long curly hair and cleavage. When I come back from the loo, two minutes later, she's in fierce discussion with the other women at her table.

'You should tell her,' one of them is saying.

'Just show her,' says the third, and grabs my arm as I'm going by.

'Take a look at this,' she says. 'You ought to know what kind of man you're going out with.'

The woman with the long hair hands me her phone. The message is from 'Steve'. It read 'ID FAR RTR B EATING WT U SX'.

'Nice,' I say, handing the phone back.

Steve asks me what it is. 'What did that woman say to you?'

'You mean *your tutor*?'

'She's someone I slept with once. I don't remember her name.'

'Only her phone number?'

'What do you mean?'

'She showed me the text you sent.'

'I don't know what you're talking about.'

'Then why don't you go and ask her?' I snap, pick up my coat and hurry out, not looking in the direction of the text woman's table. I'm on the bus home before Steve phones me.

'I challenged her after you'd gone. She was playing a game. I said I'd call her back and I didn't, so she decided to get revenge.'

'I was less than five minutes in the loo. She didn't have time to plot such an elaborate little revenge.'

'It only takes a minute to send a text. It was one of her mates' ideas.'

'She had time to fake the caller ID too?'

'Takes seconds. Do you really think I'm that devious, or desperate?'

'I don't know what you are, Steve, but I do know that you're sleeping in the front room tonight.'

'I could have any woman at that table. They were jealous of you.'

I hang up. Steve doesn't come home until two in the morning. He sleeps in the front room, as I requested. Next day, we both act like nothing really happened. He was probably telling the truth, I decide. But I can't be sure. I'll never be sure.

A week later, I'm home alone when Mark turns up. He's taken some magic mushrooms and is floating in an odd way. He offers me some but I don't fancy it. I've heard stories about people being poisoned by mushrooms.

'Probably a good thing,' he tells me. 'They make you horny. We might not be able to keep our hands off each other.'

'I've not heard that,' I say. 'Maybe you ought to go and see Helen.'

Mark's eyes focus on the middle distance. 'Helen... she's

not freezing me out, exactly but, you know Helen, she's always going to get offers. It was only a matter of time before...' He loses track of the sentence.

'Steve could be seeing someone else for all I know,' I tell Mark. 'He has the opportunity, and the track record.'

I try to talk to him about Vic, who he got on with.

'Vic was in love with you,' Mark says. 'Aidan was no threat to her but once you started screwing Steve, of course she was out of here. End of.'

He starts to say something about sex and friendship but it drifts into how Helen was upset about what he said about me that night on holiday and then some maudlin stuff about being everyone's fallback guy. I can tell he's jealous of Steve and I don't want to go there, so I try to put the conversation back on track, let Mark know how great his life is.

'You've got lots of male friends. I've only got Zoe, and she's in West Kirby. I'm not sure that's natural.'

'You're a loner,' Mark says, his eyes unnaturally bright. 'You get on with men because you're hunting for one. You have one best female friend because it's useful in the hunt some-times. More would be redundant.'

'You're saying I'm a totally selfish person.'

'We all are. Get used to it.'

I like Mark when he's stoned. He's interested in exploring ideas, getting to the heart of stuff. I like that he can be totally open about his feelings. When he makes a pass at me, he does it in such a vague way that it's impossible to be offended, or take it seriously.

'I'm horny,' he says. 'Why not? It wouldn't be the first time. Steve doesn't have to know. We're our own people, aren't we?'

'I tell Steve everything,' I say, which is a slight exaggeration.

'And I'm not horny, I'm hungry. Have you eaten?'

'No, I suppose I could...'

'I know you. You'll be ravenous soon.'

'You're probably right.'

'Let's go for a curry.'

It's late and it's raining, but there are plenty of places on the Alfreton Road that stay open until two. We could walk to one in a few minutes, but I decide to drive. That way, I can drop Mark off at his flat and get straight home without having to fend him off again. I have a lecture in the morning.

The restaurant is dead. One waiter, two other customers. I'd heard that they did good vegetarian dishes but must have heard wrong. My korma tastes of old rubber and has the texture of sludge. Mark wolfs down his King Prawn danshak with a big bottle of Cobra. The other table leaves and we have the place to ourselves, some sappy harp music playing in the background. We've run out of things to talk about.

Mark pushes his meal aside. 'Think I've had enough.'

'Me too. Shall we pay and get out?'

'Yeah'. He checks his wallet. Only a fiver in it. 'I'll put it on my card if that's OK.'

I hand him a tenner for my share and go to the loo. When I return, Mark stands up.

'Are we sorted?'

Mark nods. I pick up my coat and take a mint imperial as we leave. Mark is giving me a funny look, but I think it's the mushrooms.

'You're not going to be sick, are you?' I ask, worried about the interior of my smart car.

He shakes his head and gets in. That's when it happens. I've started the engine but not turned on the lights. Three men come charging out of the restaurant. One of them waves a cleaver. Another tries to open the driver door but, even in my panic, I have the wit to lock it. I think I'm going to pee myself. I rev the engine but the biggest man's in front of the car. I can't just pull out. Even after midnight, this is a busy road. Where's a police car when you need one? The three men begin to shake the car. The one with the cleaver waves it as though he's going to break the window, or at least scratch the hell out of my bonnet. Mark, I notice is getting out his wallet. I don't want him to give in to these muggers. I'd rather drive over the guy with the cleaver and fuck the consequences. One of the guys is shouting about money but the window is closed and his accent is thick so I can't make out all the words. Then I recognise the waiter who served us.

'Oh shit, Mark, did we just walk out without paying?'

'Give me another tenner. I only have fifteen quid.'

Seeing the money in Mark's hand and me scrabbling in my purse, the men stop shaking the car. Mark hands me the fifteen quid, to which I add a tenner. This is more than the meal would have cost, never mind what it was worth. Mark is shaking. I wind down the window a couple of inches, poke the money out.

'I'm sorry, I'm sorry. A genuine mistake.'

The waiter shakes his head as he takes the money, but the other men are grinning. This little event has made their evening. The chef puts the cleaver behind his back and gives a mock bow.

'Do come and see us again soon,' he says as I close the window.

Mark's flat is on the other side of the Arboretum. I give him an earful as I drive.

'Was that deliberate? Did you really think you'd get away

148

with stiffing people who deal with duplicitous drunks seven nights a week? Have those mushrooms turned your brain to mush?'

'I... I'd forgotten my card,' is all Mark says, and then he covers his mouth and I can tell he's about to be sick. I pull over by the cemetery and tell him to get out, quick. He does as he's told. I watch him vomit through the railings, then clean himself up with a tissue. He gets back into the car.

'I don't think that curry was a good idea,' he says.

I drop him off with a curt 'goodnight' and don't hear from him again for months.

Random

Final Year. People panic over dissertation topics, stress over whether to take modules that are all coursework or fifty-fifty split with exams. I opt for coursework: it spreads the stress, makes me feel more in control.

One of my modules is called *Nottingham Fictions*. The lecturer passes round this memoir about a bloke going to a football match in the city. It comes in a box and you read the sections in any order you like. The first and last sections are always the same, but the rest are designed to be shuffled.

'Why do you think he chose to publish it this way?' the lecturer asks.

Nobody answers. We're in our third year, but still people are afraid to make fools of themselves. Including me. Yet I wave my arm.

'Allison?'

'Isn't he, like, saying that it's a book full of memories, so they come in a random order, because that's the way we remember things in life?'

'Yeah, random.' A guy at the other end of the room nods vigorously.

Random. Half the people at uni uses that word all the time, peppering their sentence with it like the word means something profound. They don't use it the way I just used it, as a mathematical term. It's a kind of catch-all term for... I'm not sure. Aidan says it. So does Mark. A lot. Maybe it's a male thing. Only, recently, I've found myself using it too. I'm worried I've misunderstood and/or I won't notice that it's gone out of fashion while I wasn't looking. I saw Vic the other day, for the first time in weeks. When I asked what she and Liz had been up to, she said 'random stuff'.

Sometimes random seems to mean *meaningless, but not in a bad way*. Other times, it means *kind of cool, in a post-modern way*. I'm not sure I understand post-modernism. There was a professor at this Events Week thing I helped out at the other day. He started talking about *post-post-modernism*, then, after a couple of perfectly formulated, impenetrable paragraphs he repeated the phrase and added: 'You do know what I mean by post-post-modernism?' I said 'sure'. Because I may be stupid, but I'm not stupid enough to admit my stupidity. Is that random? I decide *random* is a word for anything meaningful that you don't know how to articulate. So, life is random. We're living in the *post-post-post-modern* age where everything is of equal value so nothing really matters. Yeah, right. I decide that, from now on, I will avoid the word, use *arbitrary* instead.

The others are getting on to me about my kitten, Monsta. I feed her when I remember but Steve never does and she got really skinny while we were away. If Vic were here she'd feed her when I forgot. I suspect that Monsta is a Vic substitute. I miss having a friend who's around all the time. I know there's Steve, but a boyfriend isn't a friend, and, anyway, he's still out all the time. I'm not. Since Vic and Liz moved in together, I hardly see her. I miss her. I even miss Finn and Tessa, though we weren't close. The new people in the house make no effort to get to know me, or I them. It's just a place to live.

The guy in my old room asks if Monsta's been spayed.

'There are lots of strays out there and she spends most of her time on the streets. She's bound to get pregnant the minute she's old enough.'

How old is Monsta? Less than a year, but I have no idea how much less. Mum never told me about her, presumably because she knew what getting a cat signified. I make an appointment with the PDSA, a charity who'll do the operation in exchange for a donation, rather than a fat vet's fee. Then I have her name and our address etched onto a metal tag and attach it to her flea collar.

The day before the appointment, Monsta doesn't come home. She must have sensed something, or maybe it's a coincidence. At first, I'm not too worried. She's bound to have picked up a few street smarts since moving to Nottingham. I mean to find her, not desert her. I mean to go street to street, looking for her. I mean to cancel the PDSA appointment. Then something happens to make me forget.

Steve's working late again. I reckon up how many nights he's done in the last three weeks. It's at least ten, maybe twelve. This is his final year too. He's meant to work no more than two nights a week. Bored, I ring up Zoe. She has a moan about Aidan, how little he's there for her, how he won't go to his therapy group, his secretiveness. It's all too familiar.

'He's fine when we're alone, but he's never been good in company.'

'Some people aren't.'

She asks what I'm doing at Christmas.

'Staying at Steve's. Dad's going to Barbados and Mum won't know what's going on, though I'll call her, obviously.

How about you?'

'Aidan's lot have hired a cottage in Scotland for Christmas and New Year. They've invited me. It's got to be better than staying at home.'

For each of us, it'll be our first Christmas away from West Kirby, but that's cool. We're no longer teenagers.

'Have you seen Mark?' she asks.

I tell her about my embarrassing scenes in restaurants, concluding with Steve and the mysterious text message.

'It has to be a set up,' Zoe says. 'Steve wouldn't be that obvious.'

'He was never subtle.' We discuss the numbers game. I fill in some of the details he only hinted at on Ibiza.

'Some of his conquests are bound to be resentful that he never called,' Zoe says. 'This one probably thought she was doing you a favour.'

'Maybe she was.'

'I thought you and Steve were solid.'

'I'm sure he's cheating on me,' I say, realising as I say it that 'sure' is an overstatement.

'Who with? How can you be certain?'

'Knowing Steve, it could be more than one person. He likes taking risks and he doesn't mind being obvious.'

'You're telling me. That guy could ogle for Britain in the Olympics. On Ibiza, on the beach, when I had my top off... and you should have seen the way he looked at Helen sometimes. Mind you, Helen seemed to enjoy the attention.'

'Mark was worried that Helen was playing away again.'

'You don't think..?' She doesn't have to finish the sentence.

'Steve and Helen? It has crossed my mind. Helen wouldn't, though. Would she?'

153

'Not if she thought you'd find out.'

In other words, she would. Zoe is a better judge of character than I am, which makes me wonder why she's still seeing Aidan. But we all have our blind spots.

'Helen admires your taste. She always looked up to you at school.'

'She did?'

We were at the same school for six years out of seven but I didn't notice Helen until I was in the upper sixth. I barely noticed anything other than myself. It took Mark to teach me the meaning of the word 'solipsism.'

'Have you got her address?'

✠

At eleven, I borrow a jacket with a hood on it and head out into the November chill. Helen's house is only a three minute drive away. She's in Old Lenton, by the hospital, an area full of tall, badly lit houses, each bigger than the one I live in. I park on a nearby road. Helen has a first floor room, Zoe told me. Only one first floor light is on, so that's the window I watch, hoping it's hers.

The room's occupant has company. I see more than one silhouette. I want it to be Mark. I so want it to be Mark that I ring his number, expecting to hear it ring. Instead, it goes to voicemail and I hang up. Then I dial Helen's number, which I got off Zoe. Sure enough, I see her silhouette answer the phone. I hang up quickly. All I have to do now is ring Steve's phone, and my suspicions will be squashed or confirmed. But I can't bring myself to. Instead, I wait. If I see Steve leave, I can get in my car and be in bed before he makes it back, then confront him at my leisure.

Only he doesn't leave. At quarter to twelve, Helen's light goes out. Whoever it is must be staying the night. I drive home.

Steve's already there, getting ready for bed.

'Where've you been?' he asks, and I have no answer for him.

'Walking. Thinking.'

He hugs me. 'You're freezing!'

He pours me a brandy from the stash he keeps in our chest of drawers. When I ask about his weekend, he isn't evasive, not exactly, but he doesn't have a lot to say. He makes up for this by coming on to me, and taking as long as I need before he allows himself to finish. And this release, this orgasm, this enormous feeling he gives me is enough to justify my living with him, going out with him, relying on him, for no-one else has been able to do this for me before and, when it comes down to it, what does sexual fidelity matter, as long as he's there for me when I need him to be? What does any of it matter, when we're all dust in the end?

I spend the night hugging him close to me, so close I wake up in a sweat. In the morning, as I watch him dress to go to uni, I worry that I'm being over-clingy. I've put all my eggs in the Steve basket.

I have a dissertation tutorial at eleven, but my tutor can't get much out of me. I'm dragging myself back to the car park, trying to remember where I left the Mini, when the phone rings. It's Zoe.

'Guess what?'

She sounds so cheerful that I feel I ought to be able to guess.

'What?'

'Aidan's asked me to marry him.'

'You? Aidan? Married?' This is so far beyond my expectations that, for a minute I am flummoxed, utterly unable to respond, but Zoe is too excited to notice. 'That's so... random.'

'Now look, I've thought about this and discussed it with my mum, and with Aidan, of course. I'd like you to be maid of honour.'

'Wow! Thanks, that is an honour.'

I've not said I'll do it but Zoe takes my acceptance as read and starts going on about the big occasion, when it should be and, more crucially, where. I daren't ask why she's agreed to marry Aidan in the first place. She knows her own mind, I tell myself. Which is more than I do.

Steve's not working tonight. I will be able to have a proper talk with him. We can discuss how to cope with what is happening to my mum, work out how many days to go to his at Christmas, which is less than a month away. I'll tell him about Zoe, too. That'll get him going.

I'm waiting for him to get back from uni when my phone rings. I don't recognise the number. It's Helen Kent.

'Allison, hi! You rang me last night.'

'Did I?' I am utterly incapable of making up a lie to explain myself. 'Yeah, I got your number off Zoe. How did you...?'

Thankfully, she doesn't make me finish the sentence. 'Mark recognised your number. We got cut off somehow. I would have called you back, but we were... anyway, I figured you'd call again if it was important.'

'Has Zoe told you her news?' I ask, letting Helen assume that this was what my call was about.

'Just now. Isn't that incredible? Her and Aidan. I mean, I could see her going out with him out of pity but Jesus, marrying him? What's she on?'

'She says she's in love.'

'She's known him half her life. It's not love, it's desperation. She's dropped out of uni and got that *there may never be anyone else as good as this comes my way again* feeling. I can't blame her. I was nearly stupid enough to give up Mark. He's coming to Turkey with my family at Christmas, did he tell you that? What are you and Steve doing?'

'We're going to his,' I say, as though this is a routine visit rather than the first time I'll have met his family. I'm relieved that he isn't sleeping with Helen, but I'm hardly about to share confidences with her.

When I get off the phone, Steve's home, carrying a large suitcase that I don't recognise.

'Where's that from?' I ask, as I put on the kettle to make a brew, like a dutiful housewife.

'I borrowed it,' he says, 'from a friend,' and at once I know what's coming.

'You're leaving?'

'I wanted to tell you yesterday but you were so down and...'

'You thought you'd screw me one more time for the hell of it. Who is she?'

'She's a second year. You don't know her.'

'She has nice luggage.'

'I'm not moving in with her. I'm not moving today. This is more...'

'Symbolic?' I say. 'Let me guess, she made you bring it with you because it would force you to tell me why you had it?'

'Something like that,' Steve admits. 'I'm not the living together type, with you for six months, that's five months longer than anybody before...'

'But you'd have chucked me after a fortnight if we hadn't happened to be living in the same house.'

'That's not true. I don't want to hurt you. I'm sorry it's a bad time, but there'd never be a good time, would there?'

'I suppose not.'

I am torn between demanding details of his infidelities and wanting to be dignified. This is what happens when you date a slut. At least, because I knew about his past, we have always used condoms. I don't need testing for STDs. I need my head examining for going out with him in the first place.

Steve can't move out for several days. There are notice periods, deposits to be paid. But I can't go on sharing a room with him. Next day, I persuade Jon, in my old room, to swap with me. The others are pissed off about losing the lounge/TV room but Steve's hardly there, so they keep using his room anyway. I suppose he's with his new woman. Changing rooms means that it's Jon and not me who answers the door when a guy from five streets down shows up with a name tag and a flea collar.

'He said his daughter came across her on the street a week ago but this is the first time he's found anyone at home. She was run over.'

'What happened to her body?'

'I didn't ask. You could hardly expect him to hold onto a dead cat for a week, could you?'

'No, I suppose not.'

And I have to hurry upstairs because I am bursting into tears over a cat I never wanted in the first place. How will I explain to Mum that I let her cat die? How can I explain anything to her, the state she's in?

Two weeks pass. Then term ends and everyone goes away. Except me. This is a good opportunity to get a load of work done. I need a good 2:1 if I am to hang around and do an MA, which is the only plan I can think of at the moment. As I'm driving out of the university after my last tutorial, I pass Helen. She waves, and I could easily offer her a lift, but I pretend not to see her. I'd have to talk to her. *Mark isn't just for birthdays and Christmas*, I'd have to say. *Right now I need him more than you do*.

I decide I'll work my way through the next six months. Never mind a 2:1, I'll get a first.

I'm glad to be back in the attic room. I like the view from the window. Below, the students have gone home and the area is returned to its year-round residents, Asian and Italian families, young professionals in house shares. There are a few Christmas trees but they're easy to ignore.

Zoe rings. She and Aidan haven't decided a date yet but everything's hunky dory. Before she can ask me what I'm doing over Christmas my battery dies and I decide, then and there, not to recharge my phone. I delete my facebook account. Email's easy to ignore. So are the other people in the house. Now it's just me, and my thoughts, in a high room, looking down on the world. Whatever happens is whatever happens. Random. Bring it on.

Nets

I saw him at the window again today. For a while I watched him at his computer, reading or writing, I'm not sure. Then he turned and stared at me as if I wasn't there. He sits on his swivel chair, half facing the desk, half facing the window. Now and then he raises his head. Now and then our eyes meet across the street. Or would, if I could see his eyes. I am always the one who turns away first. I go and sit on my bed, which is to the side of the window, or I pull down the red blind. That's another thing. He also has a red blind, the same shade as mine. But he never pulls it down.

Sometimes when I put my make-up on in the morning and I look around, he is already there, dressed, at the window of his study. I say it is a study, for it has a desk, and bookshelves, two plants. I don't think he sleeps there. Does he go out in the day? I don't know. Often he is in the study when I come home from university.

It is annoying, this *being observed*, yet I shall do my best to ignore it. I have a lot of work to get on with. I thought about moving the mirror, but it is brightest by the window. My mirror is round and very small. It needs all the light it can get.

This morning I get up early, raise my blind and move around the room in half light. Coming back from the bedroom in my dressing gown, I glance up and see him dart across the room, naked, to the desk. His body is thin and hairy, a little like Aidan's. Coyly, he covers his genitals with an A4 envelope as he hurries out. No glance in my direction.

The man has dark hair and is thirty, or older. He appears to live alone. Probably the house is divided up into flats, as many are round here, but I cannot see through the lower windows. It's possible he lives in a shared house, like me, or with a lover. At the weekends, he is nearly always in his study. I don't know what he does there all day — he wants me to try and guess, but I won't give him that satisfaction.

The nights are drawing in. The red blind is so thin, I fear he can make out my shadow through it. But I can't be sure. All I know is there are times I feel him watching me. Today is one. I go to the window. As I push a corner of the blind aside, I think I see his light go out. But I may be mistaken.

Outside, black clouds rush across the sky. His window is the first thing I look at when I come home from the university. Some of the others have lace curtains, to keep out intruding eyes. His bathroom (or the room that I assume is his bathroom) has them too. Do the other windows on our side have such curtains? I have no way of knowing.

The nets we used for the Tarot readings must still be around.

Last night I dreamt of him at his desk. In the dream, I sit at the window, staring. Suddenly, he gets up, a huge piece of paper in his hand. He holds it up to the window. 'WHY DON'T YOU CALL ME?' he's written, and, beneath it, a phone number. I look around for paper. I don't know what I am going to write, but when I turn back a curtain has descended between his terrace and mine, like a thin cloud, or fog. I look at the paper and read what I have written there. 'I don't have a phone.' Which is a lie. It sits by my bed, uncharged, waiting to be woken from its long sleep.

Who can I tell about this? The others in the house are second years and they all seem to be away this weekend. I know what they would say. I should have put the net curtains up as soon as I noticed him looking at me. Subconsciously, they will say, I want him to watch me. I want him. But I do not. I do not want anybody.

I have highlights put in my hair. I buy a new sweater and put on my skinny jeans. At twelve, he goes into his study and begins to work. I see him glance my way, but I am beside the dresser. He can hardly see me. I check my appearance in the mirror, then stand in the window, willing him to watch. I sway backwards and forwards as though involved in some ritual or form of exercise. I lean back like a cheap dancer, letting him take in the shape of my body. He pretends not to be looking, but every few seconds he stares in my direction, averting his eyes only when I appear to glance back at him.

This afternoon I find the nets, shoved at the back of a cupboard in the kitchen. I have no sewing machine but manage to cut them crudely to size. I stitch them up as best I can. Then I have to go into town again, to buy wire and hooks. The city is heaving with Christmas shoppers. Being there exhausts me. Everyone is spending so much money, it feels obscene. The woman at the stall gives me an odd look as I make my meagre purchase. Pushing my way out of the Victoria Centre, I see a bloke who works behind the bar with me. I haven't been in since Steve moved out and have stopped remembering to call in sick.

'Allison!' he calls out, with convincing concern. 'We've all been worried about you.'

I get ready to make up a lie, but don't need to.

'You still look really pale,' he said. 'It's a bugger, glandular fever. Do you think you'll be back in the New Year?'

'I hope so,' I say.

'I'll give your regards to everyone,' he says, and lets me go. Glandular fever, it seems, was a good choice of illness.

Back home, I put the nets up. The hooks are meant to tap in, but come flying out when I connect the wire cord. On the third go, they hold. I have left the top bit of the sash window clear so that I can open it when necessary. Also, when required, I can stand on my bed on tiptoes and see over to his room. But he cannot see me.

In the evening, his light is on but the blind is drawn. My earlier suspicions about translucence are confirmed. I make out the outline of his desk, his lamp, just as he can see mine. But now there is a further barrier between us: white, shimmering, like a thin membrane of cloud, or a veil.

Sunday. It is so dingy, I switch on the main light to work by. Immediately, I can feel him watching me. I move to the back of the room, but can't see him from my perch on the chair. He may be too low for me, huddled over his desk. I should have bought thicker nets. I'm sure that he can see through them, see everything in my room when the light is on. I have only to move the curtain aside and I shall see him, staring. I duck out of sight and prepare to swoop on the curtain, catch him. But I will not give him the satisfaction. Instead, I draw the blind. The nets and the blind: these will protect me!

My dissertation is falling behind. Today, one of the others in the house said 'We see so little of you, you've become like a ghost'. They think I go out all the time but I don't. I stay in my room with the lights off. Then, when his comes on, I know at once.

His blind is down as often as it is up nowadays. He is punishing me for putting up the nets. Or maybe it is because the nights are colder and the blind provides a little extra insulation. I know this, because I have mine down so seldom and I feel the difference. I fear he is no longer interested in me. Perhaps he never was. All sorts of doubts creep into the mind when you're in a room on your own for so long.

Where is he gone? Perhaps he has left for Christmas. I have moved my bed so that it is under the window. If I raise my head a little, I can push the nets aside and see his room. Tonight, his blind is drawn but a light is on. I can see a faint outline at his desk, working. It is enough.

The doctor came today. One of the others in the house had come to see me, something about a bill. She called him at once. He tells me I have pneumonia and must rest constantly. He told me to go home to my parents, but I explained that one of them is in hospital and the other in Barbados. Then he insisted that I move my bed away from the window. As soon as he was gone I moved it back again.

The others in the house are solicitous. They bring me soup and drinks, though I rarely want them. The doctor must have said something. You looked up from your window today and I think you saw me staring at you. I no longer see the need to conceal that I am looking. Quickly, you looked away. I felt myself become weaker. Only you keep me tethered to the world. Your presence, across the road, shows me that I am real.

I am recovering, the doctor tells me on Christmas Eve! But my recuperation will be slow. I do not let him know that I am alone in the house, that the others have all gone away. He says that I seem low, offers me anti-depressants, which I refuse. If only he knew! The reason for my low spirits is that I have not seen you at the window for two whole days!

✠

Christmas Day. The house is silent. Your blind is drawn. The lights are out. I venture from my room to the shower. The heating is on full and I savour being able to walk through the house naked, unfettered. When I return to my room your light is on. I switch on mine and hurry to the window, pulling my towel around me. You are in a dressing gown, leaning over the desk. You have a fluted glass in one hand and now and then you drink from it. You are wrapping what must be a last minute present.

I watch you do this for a minute, maybe two. You are slow and clumsy. If I was there, I would do it for you. I can feel it now, feel it down to the marrow of my bones: today is the day! I stand on the bed and pull the net curtain back so that it is behind me, willing you to look over. My bare shoulders brush against the frosted glass and tingle. You finish wrapping one present and start another, sipping at your drink all the while. Then you finish and stand up, presents in one hand, drink in the other.

At last it happens! You glance at my window and see me, staring. You smile, or I think you smile, and raise your glass in greeting. I smile back. I let the towel fall away from me and, naked, balanced on my bed, I rip the nets from their cord and pull them round me — a cold, pure white, like a wedding dress, or a shroud.

Then I draw the blind and go downstairs.

No
Depression

On New Year's Eve, I'm given the all clear on the pneumonia. Once again, I turn down the anti-depressants the doctor suggests. I've seen what they did to Aidan. The doctor offers to put me on the waiting list for counselling. I tell him I'll see someone at the university if I get depressed again. I was physically ill, not mentally ill, I insist. I wasn't suffering from depression, I was sad because my boyfriend split up with me. That's natural and, anyway, I'm over it now. Sort of. I go back to the empty house, pack a bag, and drive to West Kirby.

'No Steve?' my father asks, after a cursory hug.

'He's working,' I tell Dad, who doesn't notice that I have lost weight and become uncommunicative. Why should he? I've been acting withdrawn with him for five years. He's more interested in seeing Steve than he is me. Ingrid comments on how pale I look. I tell her it's because I spend so much time inside, studying. Then I go and hide in the spare room until everyone's gone to bed. Maybe this is how Aidan felt, back in the day.

'What happened to you?' Zoe asks when I call.

'My phone was on the blink.'

'I worked that out, but you didn't answer emails either.'

'I went off on one, but I'm back now.'

Off on one is Liverpudlian for 'let's not talk about it', only Zoe won't leave the subject.

'I wouldn't let Aidan get away with that, Allison, and he's on medication. What happened? Why haven't you been home?'

When I start crying she tells me to come round at once.

✠

Her dad answers the door. I'm too numb to react, even though it's the first time I've seen him by myself since that time on The Common, three summers ago. He's lost weight and become greyer. If he remembers what happened back then, his face doesn't show it. How much have I changed? My face has become thinner. I wear a little make-up, which I used to think was naff. My hair is shorter, less feminine, making my face look more pointy, or so I fear. But I am still recognisably the person I was two and a half years ago. Aren't I?

'How's your mother?" Bob Pritchard asks. So he does know who I am. He's prone to black-outs, Zoe told me on holiday. Maybe he has no recollection of trying to rape me.

'No different. She could go on like this for years, the doctors say.'

'Give her my best, would you?'

'Sure. She won't understand but... sure.'

He nods, then backs away when Zoe appears. I've never told Zoe what happened with her dad that day. Why? Because he's her dad. What good would it do to tell her something that would make her despise him more than she already despises him? It does you no good to hate your dad, I could tell her that. Men know they're pathetic, we don't need to rub it in. They have a strength we crave, but it's a mistake to rely on it in them. They're also weaker than us, only in different places.

'You look like shit,' Zoe says. 'What have you done to yourself?'

We talk about me for an hour. I'm not used to talking about myself, not since Mark left, anyway. Zoe sorts me out, sort of. I should get a new place in Nottingham, we agree, crack on with work, forget about blokes for a while. Sometimes all you need is a friend to spell out the obvious stuff.

'I can't believe Mark just backed out of your life like that.'

'I wouldn't have him back but Helen would. Why blame him?'

When we're done dealing with me we go on to talk about Aidan. We make ourselves an elaborate coffee with the new Krups device that's appeared in the kitchen. Bob's boat building business must be doing well.

'Aidan's the best he's been for years,' Zoe says. 'I mean, he's still on a cocktail of stuff to ward off the anxiety and depression but he's stopped self-medicating with hash and speed. He's staying off the drink. I suppose you'd say he's become a bit boring compared to how he was when I first knew him, or when he went out with you. But I love him. He suits me.'

'And the marriage thing. What did you decide?'

'That's what I've been trying to phone and email you about. The church is booked for Easter. I still want you to be the maid of honour.'

How easy is it to move from total honesty to total pretence? Easier than it sounds. I give a definite 'yes', and we go all girly and start having the sort of conversation I always imagined having one day but thought would be with someone else at an unimaginable point in the future. My ongoing depression/lack of boyfriend problems are decreed to be sorted out and my being the groom-to-be's previous girlfriend is conveniently ignored. We agree that, rather than go to my dad's, I will stay at Zoe's in the week leading up to the wedding (when, really, I should be getting ready for finals, but it seems churlish to mention this). The thought of a whole week in close proximity to Bob Pritchard sets my teeth on edge, but I don't suppose it will do much for him, either.

'I'm really, really happy for you,' I tell Zoe, even though I'm pretty sure she's making the biggest mistake of her life.

I'm saying goodbye to Zoe when her mum returns from the sales. I wave hello and start the car, for I need to get on. I have things to collect from home, stuff I put aside to take back to Nottingham. I'm going to collect them, then drop off my set of keys at the estate agent's. The house is for sale. Soon, I won't have a home in West Kirby any more.

'Allison, wait!' Mrs Pritchard shouts loudly enough for me to hear through the closed door. I wind down the window and she hurries over.

'Zoe's told you about the wedding?'

'Yes, she's asked me to be maid of honour, which is...' while I'm searching for a euphemism, Stella Pritchard carries on regardless.

'We think they're rushing into it.'

'They seem very determined.'

'You know Aidan better than we do.' Unlikely, given how

long the two families have been friends, but I let this slide.

'We want Zoe to wait until the autumn, when Aidan's probation ends and he'll have finished his current course of treatment. Aidan's parents agree. They think Zoe's very good for Aidan, but they shouldn't commit their whole lives when they've only been together for a relatively short time.'

'I can see what you mean,' I say, though I don't like the way we're talking behind Zoe's back, like my friends are patients and we're their carers. What do they want me to do? Counsel them to delay until their parents think they're ready? Both of them are older than me. Both know their own minds. I want to get away. It's cold with the window down.

'You'll talk to her?' Mrs Pritchard asks.

'You haven't told her this yourself?'

'Not in as many words.'

'You need to talk to her first. Then maybe she'll talk it over with me.'

'Thank you Allison. And you'll talk to Aidan, too?'

'I was passing,' I tell Aidan's mum, Linda. 'I should have phoned first.'

'Oh, nonsense. How lovely it is of you to drop in. Keith will be delighted.'

Linda and Keith make me feel uncomfortable. They comment on how well I look, which is a lie. They talk about Aidan as though we're related. I think they see me as the 'good' girlfriend, the one who stayed on at university, the one who dragged their son from the depths of depression. But last time I saw Aidan, back in September, he seemed so fucked up. Why have I come? I want to be reassured that he's not messing around with Zoe, that he's thought through this marriage. I'm not here because I'm being pestered to act

170

as a go-between by both sets of parents. Definitely not.

Aidan's out. Maybe I should go.

'He'll be back from church soon,' Keith says.

'They'll want a big breakfast when they get back,' Linda says. 'No eating before communion. Have you eaten, Allison?'

'A bit.'

'You've lost weight, I can tell. You'll need feeding up before you make that long drive back to Nottingham.'

By the time Aidan walks through the door, the kitchen smells of bacon, sausage, fried mushrooms, baked beans, the Full English. I am persuaded to have scrambled eggs with mine. Aidan sits down opposite me. He looks less strait-laced than I was expecting. His eyes are almost as sunken as when we first met. He is thinner than ever and his curly, barbed wire hair has started to grow longer again. It looks wild. I can't imagine him as a married man.

Anna powers through her breakfast.

'Did you say "yes" to Zoe?' is her only question.

'To be maid of honour? Of course I did.'

'Thanks,' Aidan says. 'That'll make her happy.'

When Anna's finished, Aidan and I are alone, both picking at our food. I don't know what to say, but I blunder in anyway.

'Why are you and Zoe getting married? Wouldn't living together first have made more sense?'

Aidan does that thing with his shoulders which looks like he's squirming. When we were going out it took me weeks to work out it was meant to be a shrug.

'It's just... you've been through a lot. And Zoe's a good mate. I'd hate to see her let down if you're not really ready.'

I feel like an adult talking to a child. Does being maid-of-honour-designate qualify me to ask these questions? Adding to the air of unreality, Aidan doesn't reply, merely toys with a bright yellow globule of congealed yolk that he is trying to position on his last piece of fried bread.

'Aidan?'

'Zoe keeps me grounded,' Aidan says. 'My shrink thinks she's good for me.'

'Your *shrink* told you to marry her?'

'Marriage means a lot to women,' Aidan mumbles. 'I want Zoe to stay.'

'That's not enough reason to get married. Did you think she was going to finish with you?'

He gives another languid shrug, as if to say *well, you did.*

'She's talking about getting married at Easter, Aidan. It's too soon. Do yourself a favour. Leave it until the autumn, when you're off probation and you're on less meds. Leave it until you're both sure.'

'You mean until you're sure I'm in my right mind?' Aidan asks, a trace of an old arrogance visible in his wary frown.

'No. I mean, I don't know.' I want to tell Aidan about what's happened to me, about how out of it I've been and how this makes it easier for me to relate to him. But our relationship has always been about Aidan, about his view of the world, his needs. I realise that, the less mysterious he becomes, the less I like him. He's just another fucked up bloke, trying to get a woman to cater for all his needs. The world's full of them.

'It's all right,' Aidan says, pushing his plate to one side. 'I'm going to be good to her.'

And probably he is. Zoe has known Aidan much longer than I have. Maybe the mundane Aidan, the Aidan of before the accident, is the Aidan she's marrying. Maybe she knows how to bring him back. You never know what goes on in other people's relationships. There was a time when most people were married by my age. Not any longer. This age, the university years, for lucky people like me, is a period to experiment, make mistakes. It's a time when we're anxious to define and prove ourselves, but nobody will hold us accountable if we fuck everything up. After all, we're still young and have a lifetime to repay our debts.

I don't know when the mistakes period ends. 25? 30? Aidan is desperate to get out of his mistakes period, to put all the drugs and depression and irresponsible acts behind him. But I don't think you can choose when to leave it behind. Marrying Zoe will not stop Aidan from being responsible for the death of one person and the permanent injury of another. It will not change his best friend being dead. A problem shared is not a problem halved. With Huw gone, the guilt seems to rest even more heavily on Aidan's shoulders. That must be why he goes to church.

I realise we've spent several minutes without talking, barely eating.

'Got to go,' I say.

Aidan glances at me with his stranger's eyes, then gets up to see me to the door. There's no hug, no intimate moment to indicate that we were once, however briefly, lovers. Despite this ambivalence, I kiss Aidan on the cheek. His skin smells antiseptic.

As I drive through the Mersey Tunnel, I ask myself why I didn't tell Aidan about my own depression. He would have scoffed, possibly. *Your cat died, your mum had a stroke and your boyfriend dumped you because he prefers fucking someone else? Big deal. Try killing someone.* But I'd never been dumped before. And I hate where I'm living. And my friends weren't there for me. And, come to think of it, when were you ever there for anyone, Aidan? When are you going to grow up?

Maybe the discussion would have gone the other way. We'd have bonded over how bleak the world is, how suicide is the one act that makes complete sense and only a kind of lethargy keeps us from doing it. But neither of these imagined responses convince me. I can't see me and Aidan having a heart to heart. I can only see him evading the conversation again and again.

By the time I'm on the M1 I've decided that I don't want to be Aidan and Zoe's maid of honour. However, this hardly matters, for I am more and more convinced that the wedding will never happen.

On Albert Grove, a familiar looking guy stares at me. When I park, he crosses the street. I work out who he is, and consider rushing into the house, unloading the car later. But I have never been a coward. He is older than I thought, in his mid-thirties, and wears a brown v-necked sweat shirt beneath a black leather jacket. He has a receding hairline and rimless glasses. I smile at him. He smiles back.

'How are you?' he asks.

'Better now,' I say.

He looks inside the car. 'Want a hand with your stuff?'

'I'll be all right, thanks.'

He's interested in me, concerned about me. He wears no ring and he's seen me naked. Possibly he fancies me. But he's nervous. He's long out of the learn-from-your-mistakes period and I'm definitely a potential mistake. Close up, I don't fancy him. He's too old and glasses are a turn-off for me. Maybe if he had laser eye surgery. But he wouldn't be living round here if he could afford laser eye surgery.

'I'm Robert.' He offers me his hand. I shake it limply.

'Allison.'

'See you around.'

When he's gone, I wonder if I should apologise for freaking him out over Christmas. But being open about your problems is not the English way. Later, as I'm unpacking, I see him sitting at his computer in the room across the yards. The table has moved and the machine is now side on, so that he can glance over towards my room at any moment, at any time of day.

That's it, then. I really have to move.

WHAT HAPPENED

'Maybe it's a plot to get us back together,' Mark says.

'The best man's meant to screw the bridesmaids, not the maid of honour.'

'I thought the maid of honour *was* a bridesmaid?'

He's right, so I change the subject. 'At least Aidan didn't ask Steve to be best man.'

'Who knows, Aidan might have asked him first. Seen Steve lately?'

'Not since he moved out. You seeing much of Helen?'

Mark shakes his head. 'Going away with her at Christmas was a mistake. We were at each other's throats half the time. I used to think, however bad things got between us, it was worse when we were apart. Now I think, fuck it.'

'Yeah. Fuckit's my philosophy of life, too.'

'Let's go and spend the rest of our days on the distant island of Fuckit!'

As we laugh, our bodies brush against each other. I'm living in a small flat that is within my budget. The city has a glut of student accommodation and, halfway through the academic year, rents drop to tempting levels. Posters all over town read *Just because you're a student doesn't mean you have to live like one.* It's the final year of my degree and I've bought into the advertiser's dream.

We discuss the wedding.

'How did Aidan ask you?' I want to know. 'I can't imagine Aidan asking you.'

'Actually, it wasn't Aidan who asked. It was Zoe. She said he felt shy about it, or something.'

We both laugh again, but not in a good way.

'I tried to get Aidan to put it off until the autumn,' I tell Mark. 'But he wasn't having it.'

'You tried to tell Aidan what to do? What got into you?'

'Zoe's parents were worried about everything. And they're right. She's rushing into it. Marrying Aidan could be a disaster.'

'Promise you'll stick with me at the wedding,' Mark says. 'The whole thing could get seriously weird if you're not around.'

'If they really do it at Easter, can I stay at yours? I'm meant to be staying at Zoe's but I don't think I can handle the intensity.'

'I'll get my mum to sort out the spare room for you. We're meant to be staying at a hotel for the wedding itself. Can I tell them to give us a double room together? I don't want to share with anybody else.'

'OK.'

'I'll do that, then. Better get going. Work to do.'

He kisses me on the forehead. We've sort of agreed to sleep together at Easter, but Mark remains firmly in big brother mode.

I'm glad he's been in touch more lately. Maybe Zoe told

him how down I've been. Right now, I need a big brother more than a lover. Until he gets a new girlfriend. The big brother bit only works when he's single.

February is such a crap month that they have to keep it short. Most days I do nothing but work. I am up to date with my assignments and nearly on target with my dissertation. I did drop in at Moxy's to pick up my wages from before Christmas. I wasn't upset when they told me I'd been replaced. You don't need much money when you don't have a social life.

I'm trying to be better with my mates though. I email Vic with my new address and get a friendly reply but no visit, no phone call. I see Steve in campus coffee bars a couple of times. Once he's with a tall woman who might be his new friend. I'm not bothered. He'll have worked his way through several women since dumping me. I can't believe I went out with Steve. What does that say about my self esteem? But the sex was good. When I get a new boyfriend, even if he's inexperienced, I'll be able to tell him what to do, train him up to please me before he pleases himself.

I study twelve hours a day. When I've finished studying, I watch crap on TV. I don't drink much. Sometimes I smoke a little hash to relax me at the end of the evening, but only on nights when I need something to help me sleep. I make sure I have a clear head in the morning.

February becomes March. Easter is early this year. Zoe hasn't been in touch for a while and I hope that the wedding has been postponed. I don't want to ring Zoe and put her on the spot about what's going on, so I send an email apologising for not being in touch. I ask how things are, if there's anything I need to do, explain how busy I am preparing for finals.

Zoe doesn't reply. Maybe I should visit her for the weekend. I haven't seen Mum for ages. Only what if Aidan's messing Zoe around? I don't want to get sucked in. I have to protect my head until the exams are over. I'm being selfish, I know. We all have to be selfish from time to time.

I decide that a break from Nottingham would do me good. I want to go to West Kirby but Mum's house is in no fit state. I'd rather stay at Mark's than with Zoe or my dad. I'd rather spend time with Mark than anyone else I can think of but don't want to get carried away with that thought. I text him, suggesting we meet so I can sound him out about going to West Kirby together. When he doesn't reply, I text him again. *Need 2 talk.* When he doesn't reply to that, I decide to go and see him.

Mark lives in a big old house on the edge of the Arboretum, at the end of Gill Street, by the tram line. At dusk, these streets are spooky. There's a vast graveyard on one side of the road and gothic university buildings on the other. A tram, long and shiny, filled with illuminated people, climbs the hill.

I've been in Mark's house once before. It's a rabbits' warren, with rooms on several floors. Most of the fittings look fifty years old. You ring a bell and wait to see if somebody answers the door. There are a couple of lights on, so I know that there are people home. But I also know that most people don't answer unless they're expecting a visitor. I ring the bell twice, each time holding it down for five seconds. An Asian student lets me in as she's going out. We don't exchange a word.

In the dark hallway, I check the pigeon holes. There's no mail in Mark's slot, so he's probably in Nottingham. If he isn't home, I'll leave a note. A handwritten note will guilt him out for not replying to my text.

I climb two flights of stairs. Before I reach Mark's floor, a timer turns off the light. I grope my way along a corridor. The place smells musty. I couldn't live here. I'm surprised Mark can. But he's probably got a new girlfriend. He's not bothered about this place because he spends all his time round there. Probably. I wonder what proportion of their time people our age spend being single. For some people, it's so scary, not having a partner, that they jump from one relationship to another without taking time to get comfortable with being themselves, alone.

I've so convinced myself that Mark's not here that, even when I see a trickle of light coming from beneath his door, I assume he's left a lamp on by mistake. Except, when I knock, the door opens at once.

'Allison, I was about to call you. I'm so sorry.'

He pulls me towards him into a deep, smokey hug, acting like I'm a long lost friend. It's only been a week.

'Have you spoken to Zoe?' he asks.

'Not for a while.'

'You don't know how she's taking it?'

'I don't...' I hesitate, seeing the awkward empathy in Mark's face give way to confusion. 'Taking what?'

'Oh shit, you haven't heard.'

For a few seconds, I'm relieved. The wedding's off. Aidan must have backed out. She's better off, I'll tell her.

'Aidan took an overdose yesterday. He died.'

I go numb, then shock gives way to flashes of irrational guilt. For I am sad, but I am also, in a way, relieved. Ought I to be crying?

'When did you...?'

'His mum rang an hour ago. She assumed, because of the

best man thing, that we were close. They found him this morning. It wasn't spur of the moment. He'd been saving the pills for weeks.'

'Did he leave a note?'

'I don't know.'

'I have to ring Zoe.'

'Wait. Give yourself a little time to get over the shock first.'

He's right. I have to sit down. Someone I know well, someone I have slept with, is dead. People our age aren't supposed to die.

My phone rings. Zoe. I try to gather myself.

'Sweetheart, I'm with Mark. I only just heard.'

'How could he? He didn't even write me a note.'

'Nothing at all?'

'His mum said he's scribbled *sorry for everything* on his repeat prescription pad. She said she knew what he'd done when she found the bedroom door locked. She said she's been expecting it since Huw... but nobody said anything to me. Did you think he'd do this, Allison? Did you?'

'No. If he was going to, I'd have thought he'd have done it ages ago. Not now, when he was about to get...'

'How could he do this to me, Allison?'

'It wasn't about you,' I tell her. 'It was about him.'

There's more, but she's crying a lot and so am I and we've already said all that can be said. I promise that Mark and I will see her soon.

'I have to get out of here,' I tell Mark when the call is over. 'Can we go for a walk?'

We head down the hill, along the tram line, and before we get to town, turn in to the Arboretum, which is a big, public park. We walk aimlessly, circling the bandstand, pausing by an ancient cannon, hardly talking. Mark asks about my mum. There's no change. I don't want to think about what's happening to her, so I say what's on my mind.

'I don't think I can forgive him.'

'What do you mean?'

'We haven't got the right to take our own lives. It's cowardly.'

'When you're gone, you're gone. What does it matter?'

I try to explain. 'He did something stupid, something thoughtless, but he didn't do it on purpose. He cared about what he'd done. Now he's hurt more people. He should have found ways to atone, to live with his guilt.'

'He tried, didn't he? But he couldn't forgive himself.'

'None of us can forgive ourselves. That's not how it works.'

'You getting religious on me?'

'I wish I could.'

He puts his arm around my waist and we carry on towards the other side of the park, passing office workers at the end of their day, school kids with sports bags coming home from posh private schools further up the hill.

'I spoke to his step-dad,' Mark tells me. 'Keith reckoned the healthier Aidan got, the more guilty he felt. He tried church, but it made him feel worse. The marriage thing was his last throw of the dice. Poor Zoe.'

We walk in silence until we're nearly at the park entrance on North Sherwood Street.

'I don't want to be alone tonight,' I tell Mark.

'Me neither.'

We go back to my flat, where I make us both a sandwich. We split a beer and watch the news on TV. Later, Mark borrows my toothbrush and sleeps beside me in the narrow bed. We're both in our underwear. Nothing sexual happens. But it will, sometime soon, I'm pretty sure of that. Aidan has brought us back together. We hold each other tight, all night. Neither of us sleeps much. The bed is too small and we are both preoccupied.

Where is Aidan now? Aidan was religious, while Mark is sort of agnostic. Some days, he goes on about the stupidity of all religions. Other times he says that atheism is arrogant: he believes in a vague form of reincarnation. As far as I'm concerned, there is no god, no heaven or hell. Only what we do here on earth. This is where it counts. Believing this makes the worst of our crimes worse, even more unbearable.

But what if I'm wrong and Aidan has just compounded one mortal sin with another, consigning himself to eternal darkness? How could he kill himself if he believed that? Maybe he only made himself believe in God because otherwise he would have had to kill himself sooner.

Somewhere around four or five, it is very still and quiet. I can tell that Mark is wide awake, as I am, but I ask, just in case, and he whispers back, 'Yes.'

'Do you want to talk?'

'Please. I've missed you. Tell me what I've missed.'

And I tell him what happened to me over Christmas and he holds me tight and apologises for not being there for me and for being so fucked up the night we went out for that meal. Then he tells me about what happened with Helen over the holidays and how she was always threatened by my relationship with him and what was said when they agreed to break up for good. Later I ask if I ever said about what happened with Bob Pritchard when I was seventeen.

And he says 'no'. And I tell him, all the time holding him tight, feeling him breathe. And, although we don't say it tonight, we have said it before and meant it and for once I'm sure that I do still love him and he does still love me and even if he doesn't or if he does but we don't end up staying together, we will always know that we have been loved, that we have been as close to somebody as it's possible to be and that if love can happen once, it can happen again, so the world must be a place where it's worth staying, no matter what.

This is how we pass the long, cold night, holding each other close and talking softly until it is no longer dark and we are ready to face a new day together, to get out of bed and find out what happens next.

A NOTE
FROM THE AUTHOR

Many chapters of this novel first appeared as short stories in magazines and anthologies over the last twenty years. It was only when I became a part-time university lecturer and began to look back on them that I realised I had most of a novel. I am grateful to Nottingham Trent University, where I teach Creative Writing, for the research leave during which I rewrote and added to these stories.

Some chapters first appeared in anthologies edited by students on NTU's MA in Creative Writing. 'Nets' first appeared in *Inkshed* magazine. The chapter 'Eating Out' first appeared in *Sunk Island Review 3* as 'Scenes In Restaurants'. Thanks to Mike Blackburn, its editor, for tracking me down a copy. The opening chapter also appeared in a Five Leaves anthology of Young Adult stories by East Midlands authors, *In The Frame*.

In addition to the work included here, there are two more Allison stories that first appeared in *Ambit* magazine, 'I Think We're Alone Now' (*Ambit 125*) and 'Different Ways Of Getting Drunk' (*Ambit 128*, also in Heinemann's *Best Short Stories Of The Year: 1993* and the *Minerva Book of Short Stories: 6*). Both take place after graduation and have different continuity, so didn't belong here.

Also available

The Pretender

David Belbin

224 pages, 978-1905512515, £8.99

'A gripping writerly thriller that pulls you in from the first page, and keeps you turning the pages, *The Pretender* is pacey and smart'
JACKIE KAY

From an early age, Mark Trace shows a remarkable talent for literary forgery. A gap year in Paris sees his skill exploited by an unscrupulous manuscript dealer. Hurrying home, Mark fetches up in London, working at one of the UK's oldest literary magazines. That's when the trouble really starts. Hemingway and Graham Greene are only the beginning. What starts as a prank soon becomes deadly serious. In this literary thriller David Belbin writers about originality, desire and literary ambition in the voice of a character with the capacity to deceive everyone, including himself.

Available from bookshops or, post free, from
www.fiveleaves.co.uk